AF492460

TEACHING DILEMMA

Madeline Hall

Copyright © 2022 Madeline Hall

All rights reserved.

ISBN: 9798838416254
ISBN-13:9798838416254

This is a work of fiction. Names, characters, business, events, and incidents are the products of the author's imagination. Any resemblance to actual persons, living or dead, or actual events is purely coincidental.

Acknowledgments

Team Trobregon, your support has meant the world to me. You're the family I dreamed of having, and I'll never be able to truly show you how grateful I am for that. Thank you for modeling the sort of kindness, love, respect, and acceptance that I wish I had grown up with—it's part of what made me write this book. I hope it helps others be more kind, show more love, respect, and acceptance of things—even if they don't always agree with them or understand them.

Thank you to my amazing friends that have cheered me along the way, read drafts of this book, or shared their own teaching woes with me. Every word of encouragement, no matter how small, helped me achieve this. I am so grateful for each of you.

B—There aren't any words that could sufficiently express my gratitude. You believed in me so much that it made *me* believe in *myself*! You're the Roy to my Keeley. The love, support, and grace you've given me rival any church I've ever attended. This book wouldn't exist without you, and neither would this dream-like bubble we currently have. Thank you. For everything.

Dedication

Dear Israel,

Hey Kiddo! How's it going up there? Do you get to bounce around on clouds all day like I always dreamed as a kid? Are you just one giant head looking down on everyone? I always assumed it would be one of the two…whatever it is, I hope it's wonderful. You deserve wonderful.

I remember the day I read the email informing us of your passing. I shouted, hung up on whoever I was talking with, and started crying. I couldn't believe it.

You were always the happiest kid! I swear you are one of the few kids I saw smiling no matter what was happening in class. You were so friendly, so ridiculously smart, and so nice. You were definitely one of my favorite students, although I guess now that you're in heaven, you probably see that I say that to most students…but you really were….are…one of my favorite students.

I can't help but wonder what I missed. There weren't any signs. I am so good at noticing the signs, and there weren't any! Granted, you graduated a few months prior, but somehow I feel like the decision is rarely made in one moment. At least for me—it was something I thought carefully of and often about.

I have all these maybes in my head, and I have to get them out before I explode. Like, maybe if I had shared my past with you, you would have felt more comfortable asking for help. Maybe if you knew how common these things are, you wouldn't have felt any shame. But maybe you didn't feel any shame. Maybe, for you, it was a split-second decision to end the pain or struggle going on in your head. Maybe it wasn't about shame or long-term problems.

Either way, there was preparation involved, and I wish someone could have gotten to you before you finished your preparation.

I hope this story gets to anyone and everyone before they finish their preparation.

But you'll be happy to know (and I feel pretty confident that you really would find happiness in this knowledge) that your passing saved others. The news of your passing gave those of us who knew you an opportunity to reach out to students, to tell them about the realities of mental illness and the hope and help that exist, and to tell them how much they are loved. I had more than one student later confide in me and ask for help, and I know I'm not the only teacher who had this talk with their students. Even in your passing, you continued bringing light to others.

So, Israel, I dedicate this book to you. I dedicate this book to you, to the 13-year-old me who swallowed a bottle full of pills, and to anyone who has ever struggled with or ever does struggle with mental illness. You are important. You matter. Your story matters.

Forever in my thoughts and prayers,

Ms. O

1

"Ouch!" I grumbled as quietly as I could after banging my knee on the table. Again. This was the third time, and I was getting rather fed up with myself. My clumsiness didn't usually extend to activities that involved remaining seated, but I suppose I just possess that *je ne sais quoi.*

The skin on my knee slowly darkens from an angry red to a brooding purple. Sure, I could be paying attention to the speaker at the front of the room, but then I'd have to continue questioning my life choices. This routine between my knee and the table is a welcome distraction from the reality of what I've just gotten myself into.

A week ago, I was preparing for Student Teaching. I was picking out funky dresses with fun patterns and planning on taking fervent notes on someone *else* teaching for a few weeks before carefully wading into the waters myself. I was excited to teach with the guidance of a Master Teacher—someone who would mentor me, model lessons for me, and then provide a guided release. This is the way teacher preparation has been done for ages. This method has churned out thousands of outstanding teachers.

Instead, in a massive event room with at least 50 other new teachers, I'm now preparing to teach high schoolers completely alone. With no mentor. No modeled lessons. No guided release...

I must be insane.

Not to mention the buyer's remorse I'm having over the Star Wars dresses I bought off Etsy. Somehow, I don't think the Star Wars dresses will cut it when discussing Oedipus and Odysseus. Although really, I'm not sure what's best to wear when talking about Oedipus and Odysseus. I suspect the issue is more that I can't imagine *myself* teaching it. I still remember grappling with them as a student in the recent past.

Everyone I know from college is doing the sane thing—Student Teaching. I decided the best place to learn was in my own classroom, so I accepted one of the many full-time paid teaching positions offered for Student Teachers in one of the largest school districts in the nation. I spent so much time in my teaching program observing and doing practice lessons at different grade levels I thought I probably had a pretty good foundation to be a full-time paid teacher for a whole year instead of a full-time unpaid teacher for an entire semester.

Who am I kidding? With these student loans, I couldn't afford to do Student Teaching. In addition to paying for the university course for Student Teaching, I would be a full-time teacher expected *not* to have an additional job. How many 21-year-olds do you know that can afford to pay for an entire semester of college while doing a full-time job without pay? How do they pay rent? How do they afford food? When the heck are they supposed to work, even if they wanted to?

Basically, this was the only way I could afford to continue the path to becoming a teacher. It was either start getting paid or find a new career path. I couldn't afford the Student Teaching course itself. It was a 12-unit Master's level course with Master's level tuition. In addition to paying for this insane class and working full time as an unpaid teacher, you also have to do tons of major assignments (in addition to the grading and planning outside of actual teaching hours) to obtain your teaching license.

And they wonder why our nation has a teacher shortage.

So, here I sit, trying to pretend I'm not utterly terrified about standing in front of teenagers less than a decade younger than me. In fact, during my various observations for teaching courses, I was often mistaken for one of the enrolled students rather than a college senior getting ready to start Student Teaching. I wonder how often I'll be mistaken for a student at the school I'm actually teaching at. Oh my god, what if *my students* mistake me for a student?

Everyone at my table starts shouting out, "True!" or "False!" and I realize I've missed something. I look up at the screen and see that a series of questions are being asked. Teachers are invited to discuss each one at their table and come up with an answer.

Question 1: Teachers should never give their cell phone numbers to students. True or False?

I struggle not to roll my eyes. What kind of a dumb question is this? Of *course,* you wouldn't give your number to a student. You're not their friend.

A woman with a sensible bob haircut and thick glasses says to the group, "True, obviously. Teachers should never give out their personal numbers."

A man sitting across from Ms. Practical scoots his chair forward, preparing to chime in. He wears athletic clothes and trainers. He looks like he could be a P.E. teacher or coach of some kind.

"Well, when we're playing away games, I always make sure my players have my number. There's no telling what could go wrong. And with technology these days, it seems like it shouldn't be a big deal. Can't cell phone companies recover any text messages you send anyway?"

Ms. Practical responds, "Well, that seems like too much of a risk for me."

Quite frankly, I'm with Ms. Practical on this one. There are too many things that can go wrong with personal exchanges on personal devices. I remembered learning about this great app in my teaching program that allows you to message students and parents privately without having each other's private numbers.

I clear my throat and summon all the courage I can manage in a group of strangers and ask, "Has anyone here heard of Remind?"

"Yes!" shouts Ms. Practical.

"What's that?" asks Mr. Athletic.

"It's a really great app that lets you privately contact students in a fully monitored way. The students never have your private information, and every conversation remains recorded if anything happens." My heart is pounding because speaking to strangers is terrifying to me. It's a good thing I decided to be a teacher.

To my relief, Mr. Athletic nods and says, "I'll have to look into that!" His mild enthusiasm puts my overanxious mind at ease. My heart is still pounding, but I take a few deep breaths to calm myself down.

The speaker calls everyone's attention to the front again and goes through several more seemingly absurd questions, one after another. After it appears the majority of participants have grasped the concept of appropriate teacher-student relationships, we get a 15-minute coffee break.

I stand up from my table of strangers and head towards the vendor booths. The multipurpose event room is lined with tables from various organizations offering life insurance, retirement plans, educational technology, and multiple curricula. I walk past them from a distance to avoid being attacked by a product ambassador.

I'm stunned by how many innovative programs and activities exist for students. I see a booth for a learning platform that provides scaffolded reading instruction at individualized Lexile levels that boasts incredible learning gains and flawless support for second language learners. The idea that I might be able to help my second language learners so effectively despite my lack of teaching experience has me incredibly intrigued. I nervously inquire about the other features and cost, only to learn that the program can only be purchased and used if the entire school purchases it.

I see a few more interesting programs with scaffolds and supports built in and inquire about individual teacher, each ending with the same result: either the school purchases it for every teacher, or nothing. I can't help but wonder why they even bother showing up at a new teacher orientation. What are new teachers going to be able to do to get a new school to purchase a new program? I suspect it's just torture to remind teachers there are resources that will make life easier, but they can't have them.

The last hour of the day is mine to work in my classroom, and I have been waiting all day for this. I've never had a classroom, so it's obviously the thing I'm most excited about. I wish they had started the day with key distribution instead of waiting until the end of the orientation. I realize the trainings are important, but boy are they boring. How do we live in a world with self-driving cars, but we still don't have a better way of doing orientation for teachers?

Then I remember the speaker mentioning something about hours and hours of training videos we still have to watch online, and I groan inwardly. I pull out my phone to make a note of it, then adjust my yellow cardigan and take a deep breath.

I look at the keys in my hand, and I'm pretty sure the whole world can tell I'm glowing. I'm about to open the door to my very own classroom for the first time. I can feel every inch of my skin vibrating in anticipation.

I figure I should probably document the moment, so I lift my phone up for a quick selfie in front of my classroom number. I adjust my sweater and smooth my dress again because it feels like something a real professional teacher would do before entering their classroom for the first time.

I put the key in the lock and turn it slowly. With a click, the door unlocks and I pull it open. Nothing could have prepared me for what I was about to see.

I flick on the lights in time to illuminate the horror that is my new classroom. I know instantly that this is going to take hours to set up. The dark blue carpet is stained, every desk is stacked above or below another desk, and the monstrosity is pushed all the way against the left wall. Not only that, but the room is also missing a whole wall! My classroom has an accordion divider pushed open, and I don't have the slightest idea how to close it.

"Ha!" I say to myself. I'm hoping to stay optimistic despite the horror scene in front of me. "Okay, this is just fine. A little bit of organization and we'll have this place looking like a functioning classroom in no time!" I'm convinced that if I say positive things out loud, they're more likely to come true. Don't people say if you put something out into the universe, it will come to you? So I'm putting this out in the universe: setting up my classroom will be a cinch.

I walk over to the teacher's desk at the front of the room. The oversized metal desk has three drawers, but I notice there are a few necessities missing. I open up the to-do list on my cell phone and add:

-*Ask about desk chair*

-*Ask about classroom computer*

As I'm closing the app, a movement on the floor catches my eye. I glance down to see the largest cockroach I have ever seen in my entire life. I shriek loudly, my phone dropping from my hand screen-first onto the floor. The cockroach pauses before zooming around the room again.

My stomach is in knots and my heart is pounding. I'm

sure this is taking years off my life, but I try to focus on searching for something large and heavy that I can use to kill the bug. Stepping on it just isn't an option in my favorite thin-soled flats. I can just imagine the *feeling* of the crunching sound it would make, and my whole body shudders.

After frantically searching the room with my eyes only, too scared to actually move, I discover a set of old dictionaries. I don't think I've seen a physical dictionary since I was in elementary school and my teacher let us use all the pages to create origami shapes.

I rush to the bookshelf behind my teacher's desk, grab the giant purple reference book, and tip toe slowly towards the cockroach. The bug hasn't moved in a moment, which I'm hoping means my earlier shriek killed it dead on the spot. I move as close to the bug as I can, hoping it doesn't get spooked and start running around again. I'm not sure I get enough cardio in to survive running in terror from it…

I inch forward a bit more until I'm holding the book directly over the brown bug that looks the size of a mouse. Summoning all my courage, I slam the book down as hard as I can with a little yelp of my own. I quickly hop onto the thick reference book and start stomping—just to make sure the bug is dead.

"Eww! Eww! Eww!" I say with each jump.

This is the precise moment when my department chair, Penelope Juarez, walks in to introduce herself.

So glad I'm making a GREAT first impression, I think to myself. I'm the youngest teacher on campus this year, and I really want to make a good impression. Teaching is the only thing I've ever wanted to do, and impressing my department chair seems like a worthy pursuit for a new teacher.

"Whoa, everything okay in here? I'm Penelope, your department chair,"

"Um… yeah." I can't imagine how this scene must look to her. "I sort of had a bug incident…"

"Oh yeah," she responded casually. "Bugs and the desert

definitely go together. Get used to all the desert cockroaches, spiders, and scorpions. In fact, I was actually coming to get you for the first aid training. All teachers must be certified in CPR and be familiar with first aid procedures for scorpion bites and different spider bites. Come with me, and I'll show you where the conference room is for the training."

I clear my throat and smooth the wrinkles in my white sunflower dress again. Maybe if my outfit looks professional enough, my department chair will forget that I kill cockroaches with dictionaries and jump on them like a child. Knowing I'll have to deal with the squished bug at some point, I step off the thick book and start gathering a few items for the training. Notebook, pencil, water bottle, cell phone…

I remember my cell phone flying out of my hand, and I look around the floor. Just under the edge of my desk, my phone lays motionlessly. At this point, I'm worried about anything on the floor that might move. I carefully pick it up and admire the back of the yellow glittery phone case. Maybe if I don't turn it over, everything will be fine.

"Are you coming?" my department chair asks.

I give her a quick nod and half grin, then turn over my phone. Sure enough, the screen is shattered. Most of the screen is still visible, but the disappointment that floods through me is intense. I say a silent prayer that I'll get my first paycheck before it dies completely and follow Penelope.

So much for getting an hour to work in my classroom.

2

The following day is the only day scheduled for teachers to work in their classrooms before the Back to School Meet & Greet. I haven't had many opportunities to meet my colleagues yet, but I'm grateful for that small miracle. I feel like a hot mess with all the orientation information, acronyms I'm trying to remember, and my new career as an exterminator. I would really prefer to have my classroom set up and my clumsiness under wraps before making a first impression on most of my coworkers.

One of my biggest fears is people thinking I'm too young or inexperienced for this job. I've always been the youngest at everything. I'm the youngest in my immediate family, the youngest and last of all the grandkids in my family, *and* I skipped first grade. I'm always the youngest wherever I go.

But I did spend the last four years of college working my butt off to become the best teacher possible. I spent hours studying teaching theories, research-based strategies for second language learners, and even social-emotional strategies for helping teens cope. I'm really excited to put my knowledge to use and help my students thrive. I want my colleagues to see me as a capable professional, not a first-year teacher that is also a dumpster fire.

As I pull into the school parking lot after the 20-minute drive from home, I realize I'm actually pretty nervous. I didn't think I would be nervous about working alone all day, but I am. I know I need to find the office, sign in for the day, and make it to my classroom. Beyond that, I have no idea what I'm doing. I have no idea where the bathrooms are, where a faculty lounge might be, or where to make copies. And I *really* don't want to ask.

After turning off the ignition and grabbing my cell phone, water, and classroom keys, I give myself a little pep talk.

"Okay. You don't need to be nervous," I say out loud. "You're a teacher. A *real* teacher. You belong here." I don't entirely believe myself, but it's the best shot I have at making it through the day.

I hop out of my beat-up old truck and walk towards the campus. I glance around at all the different vehicles in the parking lot. The section I've parked in is labeled "STAFF" and filled with several Hondas and Toyotas. Most of the cars are nicer than mine, but I don't see any particularly fancy ones on my way through the parking lot.

I look at the section off the right labeled "STUDENTS". It's mostly empty, which makes sense since it's technically the last day of summer, but there are still a dozen cars or so. I can't help but notice the stark difference between the vehicles in each lot. In the student's lot I see Tesla's and BMW's.

Suddenly it hits me—I will never make enough money as a teacher to own a Tesla or a BMW. At least not with all the student loan debt I had to acquire just to go to college.

I remember a few years ago when I was just starting the teaching program at my university. My dad asked if he could take me out to breakfast one weekend, and I jumped at the opportunity for a free meal (I was not prepared for how much it would cost to feed myself once I moved out of my parent's house).

I met my dad at a local Denny's, only he wasn't there alone. When I walked to the booth he occupied, I noticed my mother sitting beside him. Across from the two of them was my older sister, Elizabeth. I considered the scene I'm walking into.

"Oh man… Is this an intervention?" I asked jokingly, eyes wide. "You guys, I know I drink a lot of coffee, but I swear it's necessary. *Nobody* could make it through college without this much caffeine." I slid into the booth to sit next to my sister and gave her a sheepish smile. She looked me in the eye and gave me a sort of pitiful smile in response, but she wasn't laughing at my joke. I have always felt like an octagon in a family of circles. I just *barely* don't fit.

My mom asked about the drive from campus, which was about 40 minutes and is in no way interesting. It's the kind of question you ask when you don't want have to actually talk to the person. There's no possibility of follow-up questions, and they can't reciprocate if you didn't drive anywhere.

My sister, Elizabeth, asked about my dating life and openly showed her disdain for my lack of one. Beth is five years older than me and didn't go to college. She barely graduated high school because she was too busy with boys and clothes. And she didn't get our mom's red hair like I did. Her hair is this ridiculously angelic blonde with a magical halo hovering just above.

My dad talked about the weather and his upcoming fishing trip. We all tuned him out because we all hate fishing. I don't know how he managed to marry a woman who hates the outdoors and raise two daughters that loathe fishing.

Once we've ordered food, I'm officially locked into the event. I can't leave without making an awkward scene, so my dad used this opportunity to say, "Listen, we wanted to talk to you about your career."

My brow furrowed as I tried to figure out where this could possibly be going. Most people have told me how impressed they are that I'm willing to be a teacher. Most people have told me it's a noble profession. Of course, I hear all the stories about how much it sucks, but I think I'm strong enough to handle it.

"Sweetie," my mom began, "we're just worried about you. Teaching is hard, and you're a very sensitive person."

I'm genuinely confused about why they would be worried. Yes, teaching is hard. Otherwise, teachers would be living it up in mansions with yachts and Instagram pictures in Fiji. This wasn't a decision I made lightly.

I wondered if my face showed the utter confusion I've felt. Especially because I thought being sensitive was an asset for teachers. The teachers I connected with most as a student were the sensitive, empathetic ones. They were also the classes I tried the hardest in. Academics didn't exactly come easy for me. They required a lot of studying.

"You do cry… a lot…" my dad said, pulling me out of my tangled web of thoughts.

"Those kids are going to tear you apart," my sister added.

I gave her a look of incredulity. I thought we had an unspoken super secret sister bond where we always had each other's backs. Instead, she's telling me point blank that *I can't be a teacher*. She's not telling me I *shouldn't* be a teacher, she's telling me there's no way I could do it and do it well.

I shook my head lightly as if to clear the fog of this insane nightmare I've entered into. "Let me get this straight," I began. "This is a *teaching* intervention? You brought me to breakfast to tell me you think I cry too much to be a teacher?"

"Sam, we're just looking out for you, dear." My mom reached her freckled hand over and placed it on top of my own freckled hands that were fidgeting with a napkin. "I just don't think you'll be happy."

"Because I cry?" I clarified.

"Look," my dad interjected, "as a kid, you cried anytime I raised my voice at you. And I guess… it's not that you cry or that you're sensitive… exactly. It's that kids these days are terrible! They're mean! And you want to teach secondary grades? If you *have* to be a teacher, why not teach kindergarten? They *love* their teachers!"

As much as I felt like my family was ambushing me to tell me my life's goal is stupid, I couldn't deny that they've got some valid points. I do cry a lot. I was bullied a lot in school for being a redhead and a nerd. And not the smart kind of nerd, either. I was just the un-cool type of nerd. Now, though, I wear that nerd label proudly.

My dad also had a point about the student behavior. The teacher Facebook groups I am in were rampant with stories of exhausted and burnt out teachers. I even read about a student body-slamming a teacher for trying to break up a fight. I get that behavior is an issue. But I also know that behavior is communication. Maybe these kids just need a teacher they can communicate with. Maybe that won't be *my* experience.

"Okay, dad. I hear you. You think I'll be unhappy."

"Yes, I do."

"But I'm still going to be a teacher," and I'm resolute about that.

When the food arrived, I'm briefly distracted by the smell of fresh pancakes. Sadly, however, the dried out sausage and overcooked eggs somehow curbed my appetite all together. Or maybe it's my family and their career intervention…

"Sam, you're going to be poor. You won't be happy. You like money too much to be happy as a teacher." Again, my dad had another valid point. I don't want to be poor, but who does? And his comment about me *liking money*…Yes, Dad. I very much enjoy being able to pay my bills. We've never had much money growing up, and I think my dad was projecting. Besides, if teachers were *that* poor, there wouldn't be so many people working towards that career.

And 4 years later, here I am: walking onto the first campus of my first school as a first-year teacher.

I reach the front door and tug it open, relieved that it's unlocked. I don't have a key to get in, and I haven't exactly figured out yet how to get to my classroom *before* they open campus for the students each day. I put that worry out of my mind and wander nervously around the small front office.

One of the most beautiful women I have ever seen is sitting at the computer and smiling. She wears beautiful, loose curls and her pink lipstick further illuminates her already glowing smile. She greets me with, "Good morning, Ms. White!" She sounds so enthusiastic, I think she might be more excited than I am.

"Good morning, Amy. I think I'm supposed to sign in?" I say, unsure of myself. Amy is the principal's secretary. She's responsible for a whole host of things I don't even understand yet. She basically keeps the entire school functioning. I do know that she does payroll and handles the sub requests, so I feel like that makes her someone I should get to know.

"Yes! You'll sign in to this book and then sign out again when you leave for the day."

"Do I need to sign in every day?" I ask, worried about the long walk from the office to my classroom. The idea of having another thing to remember in the morning makes me grimace, but I suppose it's necessary.

"Oh, no. This is just for teacher work_days to make sure teachers actually show up. On regular days, you can just go right to your classroom. And if you can't make it in, you need to let me know and request a sub immediately."

I nod slowly, but find it weird that teachers have to sign in and out *only* on teacher work days. I can't imagine choosing to skip a teacher work day at the beginning of the school year. When else would teachers have the time to prepare for the year? Not only that, how do they have any idea which teachers show up or not if no one signs in on regular days? Does this mean I can leave campus when I'm on my prep period because no one has any idea where I actually am? Ugh, I have a lot to figure out.

"Thank you, Amy." I sign in next to my name, then wait until Amy looks away and quickly and as inconspicuously as possible pull out my cell phone from the pocket of my cardigan. I snap a quick picture of my name on the sign-in sheet.

It's official; I'm a teacher!

3

I navigate the maze of hallways, only turning down the wrong hall twice, before finally making it to my classroom. I grab the set of classroom keys dangling off my middle finger and search for the one labeled *202*.

Although I'm prepared for the chaos I'm walking into when I unlock my door today, I don't feel prepared to deal with the consequences of my side gig as an exterminator. I open the door and flick the too-bright fluorescent lights on. There's a bookshelf next to the light switch, so I set down my handful of keys and my water bottle.

This place is an incredible mess. I have no idea how many hours it will take me to make this look like an actual classroom. The ugly accordion wall is open, giving the giant multipurpose room the appearance of… a multipurpose room. There are no bulletin boards or decorations in either of the soon-to-be-two classrooms. The only indication that any part of this space might one day be used for teaching is the whiteboard on one half of the room. The other half doesn't even have a whiteboard.

I want to be frustrated that my classroom is such a mess

and has no windows, but I know it *could* be worse. Instead of complaining about the abundance of space and desks, I could be complaining about a lack of such. Even worse—I could have ended up in one of the 15 portables on the outskirts of campus.

It looks like there must be 75 to 100 desks stacked on the half of the room that will be my classroom, and I have no idea which furniture actually belongs here. The thought of moving all of them with my superb level of clumsiness has me hesitant, but I don't have a choice. The Back to School Meet & Greet is tomorrow morning, so I will have to do what I can with the time I have.

Sitting ominously on the floor near my desk is the thick purple dictionary I dropped on yesterday's cockroach. I have no idea how to clean the bug guts off of the book. I scan the room for options, but there's literally nothing. There are no paper towels, no Kleenex, none of the disinfectant that was so popular a few years ago after COVID. There isn't a chance in bloody hell I'm going to touch that cockroach, so I scan the room one more time, hoping some brilliant idea pops out at me. And then it does.

Next to my desk is a single, small black trashcan with 202, my room number, spray-painted in yellow. Not seeing any other options, I decide that's as good a place as any for the book. Nobody uses dictionaries anymore, right?

I bend down and carefully pick up the book, trying to strategically hold the front and back covers enough to keep it closed and not shake too much. I don't think I have the emotional capacity to handle raining cockroaches today.

I inch carefully over to the trashcan, carefully line the book up in the center, and drop it quickly. An unintentional squeal comes out of my mouth, and I jump up and down and shake around to get rid of all my heebie-jeebies.

Now that the most challenging part of my day is over, it's time to hustle with the desks. One way or another, the kids will need somewhere to sit, right? I decided to just split the desks between the two rooms and get to work.

It took me 3 hours to set up all of them. At least half of the desks have to be completely flipped over and dragged to the other side of the multi-purpose room. I do my best to arrange the desks on my side of the room into neat rows, but it doesn't look very neat. Half the of them have blue seats, half have yellow, and at least a third are uneven and tilt on one of the four legs. Still, it's starting to look like a *real* classroom.

Once my desks are set up, I only have a few more items to arrange. I have two metal bookcases, a teacher's desk, and a trash can. The beige metal bookcase near the door where I placed my keys and water earlier is almost nonfunctional aside from the top. The shelves are severely dented and broken. I want to get rid of it, but with so few surfaces in my room, I'm afraid to give it up. The bookcase behind my teacher's desk seems intact, for which I'm grateful.

It only takes a moment to realize there's nothing else to move. *What do I do now?* I wonder. I pull up my to-do list on my phone and see that I still need to find a computer and a desk chair. How do classrooms *not* come equipped with computers and desk chairs?

I don't know where to go to find these items, but I sort of know where to find Penny, my department chair. I figure she is as good of a person to ask as anyone.

As I prepare to head over to her room, I realize I don't know if I'm supposed to lock my classroom every time I leave it. There's almost nothing in here worth stealing, though. Unless, of course, a student wanted to steal a dictionary or broken bookshelf, I can't see any incentive for someone to break into my classroom. In fact, it would be less junk for me to deal with if someone *did* break in. I hope someone does come in and steal all the broken furniture while I'm away.

I leave the door unlocked while I venture to Penelope's classroom. The campus is a huge labyrinth of poorly numbered classrooms and inaccurate signs. All of the even numbered rooms are on one side of the campus, and all the odd numbers are on the other side. For the life of me, I cannot figure out whose idea it was to hang a sign that says "200's" with an arrow pointing towards my hallway when only *half* the 200 classrooms are at the end of the misleading arrow.

Getting to Penny's room isn't too much of a hassle since she's just around the corner from me in room 220. I send up a silent thanks to anyone listening that she isn't in room 221, since that would put her on the other side of campus. Seriously, who designed this place?

When I get to her classroom, I knock lightly. She's sitting at her desk, deeply invested in whatever she's working on, but she looks up and smiles when she sees me at the door. I see her wave me in through the small window, and I give a little wave back before opening the door.

As I enter, the smell of lavender floods my nose, and I can't help but feel immediately at ease. This is the first time I've seen Penny's room, and I'm completely in awe.

Her classroom has a rustic farmhouse feel to it, with desks in groups of 4 and checkered red and black fabric footstools around the walls for additional seating. Between every few footstools is a small table that doubles as a wire basket. There are growth mindset quotes around the room in chalk, and Penelope has several floor lamps to light the room.

"Wow, Penelope… your room is amazing," I say in awe. It looks like something straight off a Pinterest board.

"Thanks. It's taken years to get it to look this way."

Looking around her room, I have no doubt that she's being literal. Each group of desks has a standing miniature chalkboard with the group numbers labeled. The bulletin boards are covered in gingham and burlap bows. A bronze-colored pitcher with dried lavender stands proudly on the corner of her teacher desk. It must have cost her hundreds of dollars to decorate this room.

Once I can finally pull my eyes away from the decor and shove the envy down into the pit of my stomach, I remember why I'm here. "I had a few questions for you if you're not busy."

"Fire away," she responds with a smile.

"I was wondering where I might find a desk chair and a computer for my classroom. I don't have either and they both seem pretty important..." My voice trails off when I notice a giant iMac computer on her desk and an oversized and the overstuffed desk chair she is sitting in.

"Okay, that shouldn't be too hard. To get a desk chair, you're going to need to contact maintenance. Unfortunately, they're incredibly swamped the week before school starts, so it might take them a while to get you one."

I take a minute to process the information Penny has just given me. I don't have a desk chair. Tomorrow is the Back to School Meet & Greet, and I may not have a chair. Monday is the first day of school, and I may not have a chair. How do teachers start the school year without a chair? I was prepared for *feeling* unprepared. I wasn't prepared for *actually* being unprepared and lacking basic furniture, and I'm a little worried.

"Okay, and where can I find maintenance people?" I ask, feeling dumber by the second. I know I'm new here and nobody expects me to know everything, but I feel ridiculous for not knowing basic things like where the maintenance department is.

"Oh, you just go to the district's website and find the tab for facility services. Through there, you can submit a request for a chair," she finishes.

"Oh..." I try not to let my disappointment shine through my voice. So I need a computer to request a chair. Got it.

"And is there a way to get a computer? My classroom seems to be missing one."

"For that, you're going to want to visit our Tech guru, Mr. Wolf. He's overseeing the computers that are being distributed to students, so he's usually camped out in the library. But if you send him an email, he should get you a computer by the end of the day."

Well, there's one piece of good news at least. I may have to stand forever, but at least I can take attendance!

"Okay… one last question: how do I get to the website or email Mr. Wolf without a computer?"

Penny chuckles for a second before asking innocently, "Don't you have a cell phone?"

I push down the frustrated sigh threatening to break out and sheepishly say, "It's broken." And anyway, if my job requires me to use a computer, shouldn't it at least provide one? I'm feeling more and more embarrassed as this conversation continues.

Honestly, one of the toughest things about the journey to becoming a teacher has been all the stuff I've had to pay for. It's no wonder there's a shortage of teachers—the only people who can make it to the finish lines are the ones with financial support along the way.

"Oh. Well, use my computer," Penny offers.

With a few clicks, she's got both the facilities website open as well as an email to Mr. Wolf. She stands and motions for me to sit in her chair. I'm incredibly grateful, but I also feel incredibly awkward sitting at my department chair's desk and using her computer.

Penny teaches me how to fill out the facilities request form and the gives me the proper password to submit it. I wonder if the password requirement is there because too many teachers were requesting things. Or maybe some rogue students decided to get into the facilities website and request a thousand extra student desks and they got so fed up with it, they made the form password-protected.

The world may never know.

"How's everything else going?" she asks. "Is there anything you need help with?"

"I think I'm alright," I respond. "I just finished setting up my desks. Everything was piled up, so it took me *hours* to unstack everything and put them into rows. But that's done now, so I'm feeling pretty good."

"Oh! I forgot to tell you that Mr. Sanders absolutely *hates* rows. If he sees your desks in rows, he will definitely ding you on your evaluation."

I'm not allowed to have my desks in rows? What kind of crap is that? Where was I supposed to have learned that information? What are the other requirements for my classroom setup that I'm still missing?

"My evaluation?"

"Yeah! Every year you will have a formal evaluation from an administrator. But for the first three years, you'll be observed three separate times for your evaluation."

This sounds both exhausting and overwhelming, and I don't even know the details yet. My stomach drops, and the colony of butterflies I didn't know lived inside became active. Three observations? Even *one* observation is scary... But three? My thoughts are spiraling, and I know I need to get a grip.

"Why aren't we allowed to have desks in rows?" I ask, not sure I want to know the answer.

"Mr. Sanders believes that learning happens through conversation. Kids aren't learning as much if they aren't speaking to one another. The idea is to foster academic language."

"Oh, okay," I say. Even though I observed multiple teachers in my teacher education program, I never saw teachers have effective group conversations with students. At least half the kids were typically off-task, while the other half were unwilling to talk at all. I'm not sure how groups will foster academic language, but I'm confident it will foster an end to my sanity.

"I guess I'm going to go rearrange my desks," I say, quietly resigned. The fact that there was an expectation that I wasn't aware of has me concerned. How many other times will I be expected to do things I haven't been informed of? How will I be successful if I don't know all the things I need to know? What if my first lesson observation is just one thing after another that Mr. Sanders hates?

What if my sister was right? I really *can't* do this.

Feeling defeated, I say goodbye and head back to my classroom.

When I get back to my classroom, I spend the next hour and a half rearranging my desks into multiple different configurations. I want students to be in groups since Penny said it could effect my evaluation, but I also need the students to be able to see the board and focus.

In the end, I go for groups of six. Each group has 4 desks facing each other and two facing the whiteboard. Logistically, I feel like it's going to be exhausting to manage focus and behavior in groups like this, but if other teachers can do it, so can I.

Around lunch, the first-year-teacher gods must smile down on me because Mr. Wolf shows up. He brings with him a computer *and* a desk chair. Well, he brought me a chair. And I will be sitting on it at my desk. I guess that makes it a 'desk chair'. Once Mr. Wolf is gone, I settle into my new, hard plastic chair for an afternoon of mandatory district trainings.

I'm told that each year teachers have about 5 hours of video trainings to complete online. We can complete them anytime we want, but they do require participation and attention. As I click through each video, it dawns on me how counterintuitive they seem. These training videos are filled with the *exact things* they tell teachers *not* to do.

I listen to voice after voice read slide after slide of district policies and procedures and do my best to pay attention. Actually, that's a lie. Watching them takes about ten times longer than reading the policies. Even worse, the videos require me to click random buttons throughout them. I'm starting to think the buttons exist only to act as proof that I interacted with the material.

I can't even imagine an administrator walking into my

classroom and watching a room full of students clicking a "continue" button every few minutes in a video. If they wouldn't allow it of teachers, why do they allow it *for* teachers? I don't think anyone even cares if the information is taken in and utilized. It's as though the only purpose is to check off a box on some indefinite to-do list for the district.

I sigh to myself as the speaker on the screen tries to explain the new grade book the district has adopted, which I do not yet have access to. Another thing I'll have to email Mr. Wolf about, I'm sure.

By the time I'm almost done, it's about 4:00 PM, and I have my door propped open to encourage a breeze—and hopefully a mass exodus of any bugs. I only have one more training to complete, so I resolve to finish it before going home. I don't own a personal computer yet, and I don't know how well the district trainings will work on my cracked cell phone screen.

While I'm watching the final video, Penny pops her perfectly curled blond head into my classroom and says, "Okay, I know why I'm still on campus this late, but why are you?"

I look up at her and joke while gesturing to the screen, "I just can't get enough of the district trainings. I mean, I'm absolutely riveted!"

Penny chuckles lightly and says, "I'd much rather endure that torture than have to hang around for the board meeting."

I'm glad I'm not the *only* one who thinks these trainings are torture.

"Oh, do you go to all the board meetings?" I ask, slightly curious. Actually, I'm not sure I know what board meetings are. I start to get worried and ask, "Am I supposed to go to board meetings?"

Penny walks over with another chuckle. "No, no. I'm just speaking at the board meeting tonight about some of the policies they're voting on."

I nod half-heartedly with feigned interest. If I stop listening to these ridiculous training videos, I'll have to retake the quizzes at the end. And then I might not ever get out of here. I'm glad Penny stopped by to chat because it makes me feel a little more included, but I am worried about wasting more time on these stupid videos.

"I've been working really hard to get some of these new policies adopted. Our district has been debating them for way too long, so I decided to get things moving with community signatures and speaking at the board meetings. Tonight is the culmination of all of that, and then we will see what passes."

"Oh wow, that sounds impressive," I say. Then I ask the question that I really don't want to ask, but that she seems to *want* me to ask. "What are the policies?"

Penny's face lights up and she sits in the student desk closest to my teacher desk. "Okay, so I got tired of seeing all the things wrong with education and not standing up to do something about it, so I rallied for signatures and lobbied to get some policies passed that will better protect our students and allow parents more control over how their kids are raised."

She's passionate and her voice has a sort of excitement I haven't seen from her yet. Her speaking speeds up incrementally as she continues telling me about the policies. I pause my training video while she talks, knowing I won't be able to multitask.

"So I'm trying to pass 4 different policies with the hopes of giving parents full control over what their students learn and what morals and values they take to heart. I want to know that when my toddler goes into kindergarten, she's learning what I think she should be learning. She's really what spurred this whole thing. I knew I had to protect her."

I can't imagine what a kindergartner would have to be protected from at school, but give an understanding nod anyway. "That sounds amazing."

"It is! Alright, well, I just wanted to check in on you. Make sure you survived the first full day in your class."

"First full day *without* students," I clarify. "You might

want to check back after my first full day *with* students. Hopefully, I'm still standing."

"Oh, Sam. You're going to be fine," she says with a smile. She extends a hand and squeezes my shoulder gently.

Penny's encouragement is appreciated greatly, but I'm still nervous. She is always so happy and energetic though, it's hard to stay nervous for long. I send a silent prayer of thanks to anyone listening that my first department chair is so wonderful.

"You're going to do great on Monday! Plus, you still have all day tomorrow to psyche yourself up!"

I smile and thank her before she heads out the door.

I really like Penny, and I'm incredibly curious about the policies she lobbied for. Since I'm still at my computer and no longer watching the training videos, I do some Google sleuthing and pull up the school district's website and then the board meeting's agenda:

1. Call to Order

2. Roll Call

3. Pledge of Allegiance

4. Public Comments on Closed Session Items

5. Adjourn to Closed Session

6. Closed Session

> *6. 1 Supplemental Text Approval*
>
> *6. 2 Community Lesson Plan Approval*
>
> *6. 3 Divisive Concepts*
>
> *6. 4 Gender Identity*

7. Reconvene in Open Session

8. Public Announcement of Actions Taken In Closed Session

Curious about the items in the closed session, I click on each one to read a quick synopsis, but I get more legalese than answers. Item 6.1 has something to do with curriculum being approved. The next item has something to do with lesson plans getting approved by the community. Item 6.3 seems to be about race somehow, and the last item about gender.

I sure am glad I went to school for that English degree. It's doing me a world of good at the moment for all I'm understanding about these policies. I'm guessing someone will inform me on anything I need to know, so I click out of the browser.

For now, I have more important things to worry about— like meeting all my new students and their families tomorrow. I finally decide to grab my things and head home for the night.

4

Despite being up most of the night, I'm still awake before my 6:00 A.M. alarm on Friday morning. I really want today to be perfect, so I stayed up all night creating decorations and flyers for the Meet and Greet. I know everyone says not to worry about how decorated your classroom is, but I also know that it can play a major role in making students feel welcome and invested.

My first order of business last night was to check the the GLSEN website for free resources. One of the Diversity and Inclusion courses I took in college offered a variety of resources for making diverse groups of students feel welcome and included. The Gay, Lesbian, and Straight Educators Network was one of those. Scrolling through their site, I found a lot of helpful stuff.

One suggestion was to have a "Safe Space" sticker or poster, so I found one to print in color. I laminated it and decided it would go next to my classroom door. Students will know immediately upon entering my room that they are safe and welcome.

I also found an article about the importance of allowing

students to choose the name and pronouns they want to use. This led me down a rabbit hole and I ended up reading studies from Colombia University and the National Library of Medicine.

The articles gave some statistics for depression, anxiety, and suicidal ideation in transgender youth who weren't allowed to be their preferred gender. By affirming someone's gender, there were lower rates of depression, anxiety, and suicidal ideation. I also learned that allowing youth to medically pause the process of puberty or receive the hormones congruent with their gender identity, according to the research, prevents suicides.

The articles managed to trigger memories of my own trauma. Reading statistics and data about preventing suicides in youth has me thinking about why I decided to become a teacher.

In middle school, one of the most important things in a young girl's world is being accepted. I spent hours picking out my school clothes, styling my hair, and worrying about being an outcast. Despite my best efforts at being fashionable, I was a serious outcast. Luckily, I met my best friend, Stacy, because she was equally an outcast. We were fated to be friends.

We met on the first day of 6th grade. Finally free from the confines of elementary school, I'm sure my entire 6th grade class was thrilled with the freedom allotted to us. We were allowed to walk in hallways without being in a straight line. We didn't have to keep our hands to ourselves and sit with our assigned class. And on my first day of middle school, my first class was Physical Education.

Our P.E. teacher, Mrs. Young, had just handed out our P.E. clothes, locker assignments, and explained how the showers worked after class. Once Mrs. Young finished, everyone went to find their assigned lockers—except for Stacy and me. We were both just standing there, staring in both shock and horror at what we had just heard about public showers. We were baffled by what we'd just learned. Who in the name of Ted Lasso foolishly thought 6th grade girls would be comfortable enough to shower in front of dozens of other strangers?

"You can't be serious…" I mumbled to myself.

"Oh, I think I'm gonna be sick," Stacy said.

I jumped slightly at her voice, not realizing I had company. Standing next to me was a very tall, lanky, 11-year old with short, curly, frizzy brown hair. Her height and unconventional hair made her stand out, and I would later learn that she hated the attention. Most kids were unkind about her height and hair. Oddly enough, it's the exact thing we ended up bonding over.

My own hair wasn't quite as frizzy, but it was equally short and extremely red. Although I don't have as many freckles as my mom, I hadn't realized that red hair and freckles were something to be ashamed of until kids started picking on me in fifth grade. I wasn't worried, though. Middle school was going to be my clean slate. And once Stacy and I made eye contact through my thick-framed glasses on that fated first day of middle school, we both just *knew* we'd found our soulmates.

What I didn't know was that Stacy had been struggling with anxiety and depression for years. Her parents were divorced, so Stacy was forced to switch back and forth between her parents a lot. She lived mostly with her mom, but her parents shared custody of her. She preferred being at her mom's though, because her dad would bring home new women way too often. Stacy got tired of all the obviously homeless drug addicts her dad would eventually let move in. She also hated that, just after a few weeks, like clockwork, the fighting would get so bad that the new woman would pack her bags and finally leave. Stacy's dad had a temper, and few women put up with it once he ran out of drugs.

Stacy's mom wasn't much better. She was a functional

alcoholic working temp jobs wherever she could find them. She stuck to temp jobs because she couldn't reliably show up to a regular job. She would make it to work most days, but it really just depended on how hungover she was from the night before. If she'd taken her Excedrin and drank enough water, she would pull herself through the next day of work. If not, she'd stay home and binge drink more.

Whether or not Stacy's mom went to work was mostly irrelevant. The only consistent thing in Stacy's life was her mom's blackouts. She would typically be passed out drunk on the couch by 6 or 7 every evening. In lieu of caregivers, Stacy would make herself a frozen microwave dinner most nights.

One particularly rough night she told me about had her cleaning up her mom's vomit after finding her lying naked in it just outside the shower. Stacy had to clean her mom, dress her, and then clean the vomit off the bathroom tile.

Naturally, it took a while for Stacy to ever mention her family. For the first full year of our friendship, she avoided any opportunities to talk about them or have me over. We could never hang out at her house, and she would never tell me why.

Instead, we spent all our time in my bedroom trying to mimic YouTube makeup tutorials and learn TikTok dances. My mom would pop her head in every few hours to offer snacks and terrible puns. We would roll our eyes and make fun of her inability to be "cool". And Stacy always had to go back home to her mom.

Despite our dramatically different home lives, we both had the same invisible status once we were at school. Girls made fun of both of us because of our hair, our shyness, anything they could come up with. We never did get used to being picked on.

And then, one October day in 7th grade, everything changed.

I will remember that excruciating day for the rest of my life.

Stacy and I hadn't seen each other in about a week. We didn't have any classes together in 7th grade, and whenever Stacy was staying at her dad's, she tended to miss more school. Not seeing her for a week at a time wasn't unheard of. She didn't have a cell phone either, so we were used to going days without talking.

It was a dreary Thursday morning. It had rained hard all night and only stopped a few moments before we had to leave for school. I remember the loud rain had kept me up all night, so I was cranky and fighting with my sister that morning. When I finally made the 20-minute walk to school, Stacy was the last thing on my mind.

And when my mom pulled me out of school before lunch that day, I still wasn't thinking about Stacy. Instead, I was thinking about how the smile on her face didn't look genuine. I was thinking about how money was usually pretty tight in our family, how mom worked long shifts as a manager at the local grocery store, so getting time off to pick me up wasn't easy.

She took me to our local Target and told me to pick out a journal. I wasn't really into writing, so I thought it was weird. After we picked out a journal, Mom took me to the stuffed animals in the toy section and insisted I pick out a massive stuffed animal. I could have any stuffed animal I wanted, but it had to be one of the biggest ones they had. Another very, very bizarre occurrence. By the time we were checking out, I was incredibly suspicious.

When we got home, she told me to sit down on our big, gray, worn-out couch and sat next to me. She wrapped her thin arm around my shoulders and put the stuffed animal down next to me.

"Baby girl, I have to tell you some really sad news. But before I tell you, I want you to know that it's okay to feel however you feel about it. That's why we went shopping. I wanted you to have a stuffed animal to comfort you, and a journal for you to write about what you're feeling. You're not alone, and you will make it through this. "

The invisible hand that lives in my abdomen chooses this moment to grab my stomach and squeeze as hard as it can. My whole body tensed.

A moment passed.

I saw a deep anguish in my mom's face that I've never seen before, and I was scared.

Another moment passed, and she's still not talking.

"Mom?" I asked tentatively.

She cleared her throat. "Stacy passed away last night."

My eyebrows shot up and practically touched my hairline as I asked incredulously, "...what?" My mouth has gone dry and all the blood has drained from my face... Maybe that's why I started to feel dizzy.

"She passed away last night. Apparently, she had been having some trouble for quite a while and she decided to end her life."

"She killed herself?"

My mom nodded, her eyes regarding me intently.

I couldn't wrap my head around the information. My best friend, Stacy, killed herself? My best friend who made up silly rhymes to make me feel better when I got teased?

"Roses are red, Violets are blue. Sam's a badass; why aren't you?"

My best friend who would secretly try to make me laugh embarrassingly loudly in the middle of tests. My best friend who gave the best bear hugs ever... killed herself?

What does it take to be willing to end your own life? I couldn't relate to that feeling, but I knew I would spend the rest of my life trying to understand it.

A weight I didn't know was sitting above me, dropped onto my chest, and I crumbled into my mom. The sobbing consumed my entire body. I felt it shudder involuntarily with each new sob that ripped through my chest. The sadness started to overwhelm me, and I began heaving in a way that gave "ugly crying" a whole new meaning.

My mom held me and rubbed my back without saying

anything. Each breath grew shorter and quicker, and my head began to spin. My face felt like a thousand pins and needles were pressing into it. Someone seemed to turn the lights off, and I'm so confused. I thought I might be dying.

And that's when my panic attacks started. That's when my anxiety went from manageable and occasional to ever-present. That's also when I became outraged at all the adults in Stacy's life who didn't notice she was hurting. But really, the outrage was more at myself. I knew she was hurting, but I didn't know it was this bad. How could I have known?

Stacy's parents obviously hadn't been qualified to care for her, given that she resorted to ending her life. The teachers who encountered Stacy at school weren't much more supportive. They often gave her a hard time for her tardies and absences. She didn't know how to explain that her attendance was beyond her control, so she would skip school often just to avoid the nagging. She knew she was supposed to be in class. She didn't need someone else to remind her while she was stuck at home caring for her inebriated mother.

Stacy didn't have anyone else; just her teachers and her parents. And when her mom was passed out and needed someone to get her into her bed and make sure she had food and Excedrin, and when her dad disappeared on drug binges for days at a time, Stacy really had no one.

She had no one to remind her to charge her phone and set her alarm for school. She had no one to drive her the two miles to school, and no one to do her laundry or make sure the shampoo and conditioner were stocked. As a result, school wasn't always a priority for Stacy, and her teachers made sure she knew how much they didn't like it.

So, I decided to become a teacher. More specifically, I decided to become the kind of teacher that should have taught Stacy. And now that I have an actual teaching job, I don't know exactly what I need to do to make that happen, but I have some ideas.

I'm going to be the teacher that welcomes chronically absent students back with unbridled enthusiasm. I'm going to be the teacher that says every student's name as they enter class everyday so they know they're not invisible. I'm going to shake every student's hand each day, make eye contact with them, and tell them how happy I am that they made it to class. I'm going to notice the students who are quiet and hurting. I'm going to make my room a safe space for every student.

And that's why I stayed up so late last night creating flyers. I made sure there were websites and phone numbers for things like the Suicide Hotline and the Trevor Project—organizations existing to prevent suicides. I also include my contact information, my philosophy of teaching, and my class expectations. I'm hoping this will set a foundation of trust and mutual respect with the families I would meet at the Back to School Meet & Greet that's happening today.

Once I arrive on campus and find a suitable parking spot, I realize I have no idea how I'm going to get all the stuff from my car to the classroom in the middle of the giant labyrinth that is our school. I hoist my laptop bag over my shoulder, grab the emergency Ikea bag I keep in my trunk, and I load it with my new classroom posters, a staple gun I had buy, a few reams of paper for my first sets of copies, and a variety of snacks for the Meet and Greet. After hoisting the Ikea bag onto my other shoulder, I grab the case of water out of my trunk.

Loaded down like a pack mule, I carefully make my way to the front entrance. My steps are slow and labored, and my arms and face are turning red from the strain. Just as I've hobbled to the front door and began to wonder how I'd open it, Penny walks up behind me.

"Ooh, girl!" she says with a hint of awe in her voice. "You're going to have to get yourself a rolling cart."

"That's a thing?" I ask. Why hadn't I thought about that?

Penny smiles and nods as she holds the front door open for me. I make a mental note of it on my exponentially growing shopping list. She reaches for the case of water in my hands and walks with me to my classroom.

5

Once I'm in my classroom, I pull the only table in the room near the door and line it with a vinyl tablecloth I picked up from the dollar store. I then set out all the items from my Ikea bag. There's the stack of flyers on the left, bottled water with cardstock tags that read "Welcome Families," and I have a Costco tray of cookies and a few bags of chips on the right.

About an hour later, my first visitors arrive. When the first parent and student duo walked in, I have my head deep inside a Chromebook charging station, trying to understand the inner workings in preparation for student use next week. I hear the knock on the propped-open classroom door. In an effort to hastily remove myself from the awkward position, I bump my head on the corner on the way out.

"Ouch!" I yelp at the stinging pain. I immediately start rubbing the spot on my head and try to focus.

"Oh, are you okay?" a woman asks with concern in her voice.

It's the absolute worst when someone sees your mishap *and* asks if you're okay. Somehow, it makes it more embarrassing, like reliving the painful stupidity.

"I'm alright," I respond with a forced smile. "I'm Ms. White! So nice to meet you!" I say, putting my hand out awkwardly to shake the woman's hand. I'm really hoping we can pretend she didn't see me hit my head for the rest of the conversation.

She shakes my hand briefly, introduces herself as Deb, and tells me how much she's looking forward to the new school year. I glance at the silent teenager beside her and ask, "What's your name?"

"Jax," they respond without looking at me. Jax is a few inches taller than me, though most students probably are. Jax's black hair is shaved close to their head on one side with green-tipped hair parted carefully on the left to allow their hair to drape perfectly to the right. Jax has an eyebrow ring, a piercing at the bridge of their nose, another inside their upper lip, one more on their lower lip, and large black plugs in each ear.

"That's actually what I wanted to talk to you about," Jax's mom says. "Jax's school records say their name is Brianna. They prefer the name Jax and use 'they' and 'them' pronouns. We want to make sure Jax's teachers are aware ahead of time."

My face lights up with understanding and I tell the woman, "Oh, thank you so much for telling me! I'll make a note of it on my roster. Jax, are you excited for school to start?"

"No, not really..." they trail off.

"Jax isn't a big fan of school, actually. They have really bad anxiety and that keeps them from participating and sometimes attending school." I notice how flawlessly Jax's mom has swapped gender-specific pronouns for Jax's preferred pronouns. She never slips up or seems inconvenienced, and I'm immediately impressed with her. Impressed, or intimidated... I'm sure to mix up Jax's pronouns myself.

"Ooh," I say with concern. I summon my best 'mom voice' and say, "Well, I'm so happy you're here, Jax. This classroom is a safe space for everyone and I have actually struggled with anxiety my whole life. So, if you ever need a safe place to have your panic attacks or someone to talk to, please feel free to stop by my room anytime."

Jax's mom's face lights up while I'm talking and she says, "See, Jax! You're going to be fine. You already have some awesome teachers."

My face burns red in embarrassment. I wonder if it's appropriate to tell a student I have anxiety. I begin to worry I might get reprimanded. But the mom did seem really happy when I mentioned it. As a new teacher, I have to learn what to share and keep private by trial and error. Not a fan.

Jax and I chat a bit about their schedule and I hand them one of my flyers before we say our goodbyes. Once they leave, the biggest smile covers my face. My grin is ear to ear and I don't even try to hide it.

I did it! I survived my first family interaction! I'm so proud of myself that I start to do a little dance, holding up the index finger on each hand and turning myself around. I'm quickly, and unfortunately, interrupted by another parent.

I'm really glad I have all these embarrassing moments to reflect on today.

The new group to wander into my room is a family of four. The mother is poised and stands confidently in a beautiful blue and white maxi dress. Her arms, hands, legs, and neck are covered in body art. The piercings adorning her face add an almost glittering quality. She pushes a large black stroller with a sleeping baby. The father is short with an inconvenienced look on his face. I see his shaved head and irritated expression just above the even shorter girl standing in front of him.

"Hi, welcome!" I say with too much enthusiasm for this stoic group. "My name is Ms. White. It's nice to meet you." I again shake hands with each of the parents and comment on the adorable sleeping baby, hoping to get either parent to crack a smile. Neither does.

The student, whose name turns out to be Marie, lets her eyes fall on everything around the room that *isn't* me. I'm starting to notice a pattern in the students. Are all teenagers this weird about making eye contact?

I see her looking at the snacks and water. "Do you want something to eat or drink? Please, help yourself. That's what it's there for," I encourage with another smile. I ask if she's excited for school to start and get the expected, "No, not really" response. I'm starting to think I need more discussion questions in my tool belt. What am I supposed to talk about now that I've asked my *only* question?

At that moment, Marie's mother, completely deadpan, looks straight into my soul and demands, "Who decided to put Marie in Honors English?"

I'm completely caught off guard. Judging by her expression and the confidence she's radiating, I infer that she's not joking. I also infer that she is *pissed* about her daughter being in an honors class.

"What do you mean?" I ask, dumbfounded. Definitely dumbfounded. Wasn't making it into an honors class a *good* thing? Isn't that something parents push their kids towards and then celebrate when it happens?

"I want to know who decided she should be in an honors class."

My stomach drops. I can feel my anxiety slowly creeping in. My heart is beginning to race and adrenaline has started to course through my veins. I try to think of an appropriate response to a parent upset about their child being in an honors class.

Is this really happening?

"I'm sorry," I begin. "I don't actually know anything about scheduling. I'm guessing her last English teacher believed she was capable and would do well. But don't worry, I will do everything I can to make sure Marie is successful."

"She better be," the mom mumbles while grabbing a flyer. She turns and walks out of the room without saying goodbye. Her husband and two kids trail behind her. I didn't see a single one smile the whole time they were in here. I wonder what this will mean for the school year with Marie as a student.

Once they're out of the classroom, I sit in a student desk for a few minutes to practice some breathing exercises. I remember my therapist's instructions to take a deep breath through my nose for 4 seconds, hold it for 7 seconds, then let it out through my mouth for 8 seconds. I repeat this until my heart rate has slowed and the dizziness has settled down.

I've gotten really good at managing my panic attacks over the last few years, and I'm grateful I put the work. I'm not sure I would have made it this far otherwise. I can't imagine having a panic attack in front of a parent or student. I realize it will probably happen at some point. My whole body shudders just thinking about it.

I head over to my desk and start a spreadsheet for student notes. I write the name of the two students I've met so far and the info I've learned. Next to Marie's name I write, *"Honors?"*

To my disappointment, only a few more families actually make it into my room to say hello during the rest of the day. I guess there aren't many parents that can take a day off of work to meet their student's teachers. Which is just as well since I won't remember any of them anyway. I end up using most of the time to prep for my lessons for the first week of school.

I don't have the first clue about what to teach during the first week of school. No one has said anything about what they're teaching or anything about what I'm *supposed* to be teaching, so I decide to Google activities for the first week of school. While doing so, I come across an amazing website full of teacher created lessons and resources. The website is called Teachers Pay Teachers.

I scour the website looking for anything free and come across an assignment for Six-Word Memoirs. There are a few Six-Word Memoir books that I've fallen in love with over the years, so the assignment seems particularly appealing. The idea is to write your whole life story with exactly six words.

I immediately add the free file to my Google Drive account and open it up. It turns out to be one slide that says:

Write a sentence about yourself using just 6 words.

I'm so underwhelmed, I think I might fall out of my chair. Which would be a terrible thing because I don't know how my health insurance works or when it kicks in.

One slide.

One sentence.

I sigh a little too loudly in frustration and delete the poorly made activity. I immediately check for the email asking me to rate the product and give it one star. Unfortunately, if you give a product less than 3 stars, it requires the customer to write a review. There was no way I was going to waste *additional* time on this, so I clicked cancel and clicked out of the browser. I resign myself to the fact that I'll be creating this from scratch like the rest of my lessons this year, and start searching for engaging slide deck themes.

I'm completely absorbed in lesson planning when it's finally time to leave. I feel a little deflated that only a few families stopped by, but I'm happy I got a chance to meet some students. I clean up the few items I set out for visitors and head home.

6

On Sunday, the night before the first official school day, I tuck myself into bed after an appropriately hefty dose of melatonin and my new phone. I found time to replace it over the weekend, but not without borrowing money from my parents first. Teachers in my district only get paid once a month (on the last day of the month to make things even more convenient), and that means new teachers have to work for a whole month before they even get their first paycheck.

I scroll through social media to kill time until the melatonin kicks in. I check Facebook Marketplace for stuff that might be useful for my classroom, even though I don't have any money. Then I get the idea to search for teacher groups in my district. I come across a few and quickly click *JOIN GROUP* on one of them. A screen pops up with the group's rules, and it's mentioned that the group is not moderated. I find this odd, but click the button to acknowledge the notice. And just like Alice in Wonderland, there is no going back.

The group is riddled with posts complaining about various things. One teacher complains about her class sizes and wonders if it's a fire hazard. She apparently has 45 students in her American Sign Language class periods this year and only 30 desks. I can't imagine what she will do with 15 students who don't have desks.

Another teacher rants about the mandatory district trainings we have to do online. For fun, I scroll through the comments of this post. It looks like most of the teachers in my district feel the same way about the trainings that I do. A few teachers suggest potential narrators for some of the videos, and others begin to post new memes about the trainings. Some comment on not completing the "mandated" district training in years.

I see another teacher complaining about evaluations. She argues that evaluating teachers when we are short-staffed, underfunded, and our classrooms are overcrowded is not only absurd but also 'traumatizing' to teachers. The invisible hand in my gut is starting to clench, and I'm replaying the diner scene with my family in my head.

I continue scrolling until I'm well versed on the issues with our health insurance. Apparently, if an insurance company doesn't pay its providers, the providers stop providing services. Multiple teachers mention being in collections for medical bills the health insurance *didn't* pay.

How does this district manage to get teachers to work for them? How on earth do they stay staffed? I guess they don't, which is how I ended up here. If any of this were advertised, teachers would never accept a job in this district. To be completely honest, I'm not sure if I would have either.

I'm starting to realize that the more time I spend reading posts in this group, the more my mental health is going to suffer. I'm learning a lot more than I expected about a district with a lot more issues than I could have predicted. My mind is swirling with worries about all the things I've read.

I get ready to swipe out of the app, but I pause when I notice a post from Penny.

Penny J: Thank you to everyone who worked so hard to get these new policies put in place. Our kids deserve to be safe and protected. This year, we've shown them that they can count on our unwavering support. That's what Shipman parents are all about!

Intrigued, I click on the picture next to her name to pull up her full profile. I don't really know anything about Penny other than she's the cheer coach, the English Department Chair, and she has an unnatural obsession with Jane Eyre.

Her profile page loads and her cover photo is a beautiful field of pink and purple flowers with a perfectly clear, blue sky. A Bible verse scrolls across the bottom of the serene photo: *"He was pierced because of our rebellions and crushed because of our crimes. He bore the punishment that made us whole; by his wounds we are healed"* Isaiah 53:5. I sort of wondered if she was religious when she mentioned her policies to me, but now I know she is.

I click on her actual profile photo to enlarge it. I'm looking at the cutest family photo I've seen in a while. Penny stands in a beautiful red, white, and blue sundress. She wears a straw hat over her perfect, short curled blonde hair and looks to be holding it on her head while laughing with her mouth wide open in genuine glee. She appears to be laughing at the little girl and the dog in the photo.

The little girl stands in front of her with one hand gripping the hem of her mom's sundress, and the other gripping an empty ice cream cone. Her sundress matches her mom's, as do her curls. She looks to be about 2 or 3 years old, and her expression is one of incredulity as she stares at her empty ice cream cone. A black and white dog stands next to her, licking the ground.

A man, presumably her husband, stands off to the side of Penny with his hand resting on her back. He's wearing cargo shorts and white shirt with embroidered fireworks. In the background of the picture is an American flag, just below the sign for the local community church.

The photo is beautiful and makes me genuinely smile. After clicking out of the photo, I scroll down Penny's page and see what she's posted for public viewing. There are a lot of church postings. One for a women's luncheon, several inspiring Bible verses, and even an invitation to her new play group, *"Tots for Christ"*.

Once I make it back to her original post in the teacher's group, I can't help but read some of the replies. I didn't realize Penny was so religious, and now I feel a little awkward. I'm not religious myself, but I always feel like I'm somehow disappointing the religious people around me by not believing in… *anything*. My parents both forced me to go to church as a kid, so I stopped going once they gave me the freedom to choose.

I click on the button to read the comments, and I'm shocked by much of what I read. Everyone is either incredibly angry and cruel, or… extremely religious. People either hail her for following Jesus' commands, or they accuse her of turning our schools into the *1984* novel.

I'm starting to think I should probably know what these policies are. I was working really hard to not get involved. Every advisor I ever had in college told me that new teachers needed to keep their heads down. If we speak up or have an unpopular opinion, we're less likely to get tenure. No tenure, no paycheck. And until you get tenure, your administration can let you go at anytime without reason.

Once we get tenure, it's much more difficult to fire us. Schools are usually required to go through an improvement plan and a lot of documentation once a teacher has obtained tenure. So, as a new teacher without it, I've decided to do *just* what my advisors advised. I will keep my head down.

I think that's why I've avoided researching the policies until now. I can't have an opinion about something I'm unaware of, and there's nothing I can do to make a difference anyway. If I want to stay employed, I follow the district policies.

I decide to do a quick search across the district's website and board agenda items to read up on the policies again before my melatonin has me out cold. I find links to the original policies and begin to read:

An act relating to parental rights in education; requiring district school boards to adopt procedures that comport with certain provisions of law for notifying a student's parent of specified information; requiring such procedures to reinforce the fundamental right of parents to make decisions regarding the upbringing and control of their children in a specified manner...

I have seen a lot of these types of bills introduced over the years, but they never actually pass. Once the pandemic hit, Americans were forced to remain inside with nothing but social media and documentary series on streaming platforms. As a result of that and some other national atrocities, Americans were forced to start reconciling with their uncomfortably racist past. Unfortunately, not everyone was on board.

Parents started deciding they wanted the right to determine what version of history and reality they wanted their children taught. Now, these types of bills get proposed so often, it's no longer considered news. That must be why I hadn't heard anything about this before signing my contract.

I read on: *...prohibiting the procedures from prohibiting a parent from accessing certain records; providing construction; prohibiting a school district from adopting procedures or student support forms that prohibit school district personnel from notifying a parent about specified information or that encourage or have the effect of encouraging a student to withhold from a parent such information; prohibiting school district personnel from discouraging or prohibiting parental notification and involvement in critical decisions affecting a student's mental, emotional, or physical well-being; providing construction; prohibiting classroom discussion about sexual orientation or gender identity in all grade levels or in a specified manner; requiring certain training developed*

> *or provided by a school district to adhere to standards established by the Department of Education; requiring school districts to notify parents of healthcare services and provide parents the opportunity to consent or decline such services;*

The constant use of semicolons is making my head spin and making the content harder to comprehend this late at night. I'm sure the melatonin isn't helping either. I keep reading anyway:

> *…requiring school districts to provide parents with certain questionnaires or health screening forms and obtain parental permission before administering such questionnaires and forms;*

During the pandemic, students worldwide were forced to learn from home to maintain social distancing and minimize the number of COVID-19 infections. When that happened, the world's collective trauma was documented through health surveys and questionnaires administered by schools. They found significant increases in anxiety, depression, suicidal ideation, and abuse. They found those numbers were even higher among girls and members of the LGBTQ+ community.

Again, not everyone in the world agreed. Some people still don't believe in mental health. Many religious and conservative families were upset to find their kids were taking surveys about subjects they *themselves* had never even spoken to their children about. Like the sitting president at the time who believed the pandemic would go away if people stopped getting tested, families believed if they didn't talk about it, it didn't exist. If you don't acknowledge mental health, then you don't have to be held accountable for your own choices and actions and how those may impact people around you.

Is that what I'm doing by not making sure I'm informed about these policies? Am I ignoring the issues so I don't have to feel accountable for my action—or inaction—around them? Maybe if I don't know what the policies are, then I'm somehow less responsible for fighting against them…

My eyes scan the rest of the bill's introduction: *...requiring school districts to adopt certain procedures for resolving specified parental concerns; requiring resolution within a specified timeframe; requiring the Commissioner of Education to appoint a special magistrate for unresolved concerns; requiring school districts to bear the costs of the special magistrate; requiring the State Board of Education to adopt rules; providing requirements for such rules; authorizing a parent to bring an action against a school district to obtain a declaratory judgment that a school district procedure or practice violates certain provisions of law; providing for the additional award of injunctive relief, damages, and reasonable attorney fees and court costs to certain parents; requiring school district to adopt policies to notify parents of certain rights; providing construction; requiring the department to review and update, as necessary, specified materials by a certain date; providing an effective date.*

I do a double-take when I read the part about schools being required to fund all of this. Most districts are understaffed as it is—and that began before the pandemic hit. Now, the district has to find a way to fund more people spending more time drafting new policies, find a way to fund new positions to enforce said new policies, and provide money to anyone who decides to sue them over said policies.

And people wonder why there isn't more money to pay teachers?

I can feel the melatonin kicking in. My entire body feels heavy and I can hardly keep my eyes open. I know I need to get some rest if I'm going to survive my first day with students, so I close all of the open apps on my phone. I'm about to set it down on the table next to me when I hear a ping to alert me that I have a new email. I open my email app to see I have one from my principal, Mr. Sanders. It reads:

Welcome back, Shipman staff!

I just wanted to wish everyone a great first day of

school. Several of you have been asking if we will start our Monday Morning Meetings up again, and that answer is YES. We have some important announcements about some new policies that will need to be implemented the first few weeks of the semester.

I will see you all in the cafeteria tomorrow at 7:00 A.M. sharp with coffee and bagels. Don't forget to bring your own breakfast, too.

We've got this, Shipman!

Your Captain,

Mr. Sanders

Well, it sounds like my curiosity might be satisfied during the meeting tomorrow morning. It sounds like we'll be learning about the ramifications of the bill on our first day of school. What a way to start my career.

7

When my alarm goes off Monday morning, I immediately hit snooze. Once the other 7 alarms I set for the following 10 minutes also go off, I begrudgingly decide to get up and get ready.

It's finally the first day of school, and I can feel butterflies taking up residency in my stomach again. I'm reminded of all those first-day-of-school photos my mom used to force my sister and me to pose for every year. In the weeks leading up to the first day of school, she would spend hours creating the perfect backgrounds with oversized flowers, balloons, and giant numbers for the different school years. She would make each of us hold up a chalkboard with a bunch of random statistics: our age, favorite color and foods, etc. Eventually, my sister and I refused to wear the matching outfits anymore, and the pictures finally ceased.

I wonder what a teacher's chalkboard of stats would look like for a first day of school photo. I wonder what *my* chalkboard of stats would look like for today.

Years Taught: 0

Money Spent on Education: $120k

Money Spent on Classroom Supplies: $400
Yearly Pay: $42k
Times I've Thought About Quitting: 2

I choose my favorite non-dinosaur themed dress and comfortable forest green flats for my first day outfit. My dark red hair, that I now keep long, is carefully pulled back in a French braid. I've even found cute dangly cactus earrings to match the succulent pattern on my dress, and I even attempted to put on eyeliner this morning. Despite poking myself in the eye twice, I'm feeling confident. Absolutely terrified of pretending like I should have authority over teenagers, but ready to tackle my first day of teaching nonetheless.

I'm able to hit the Dutch Bros. drive through on the way to work so that I can, indeed, bring my own breakfast to the meeting. I think about the last paragraph of Mr. Sander's email from last night, *"I will see you all in the cafeteria tomorrow at 7:00 A.M. sharp with coffee and bagels. Don't forget to bring your own breakfast, too!"* You'd think he would have at least sprung for some donuts for his staff on the first day of school for the surprise meeting he informed everyone of *last night*. Or, he could have reworded it so it didn't appear he was intentionally sounding like he was offering breakfast to the whole staff.

I make it into the cafeteria right at 7:00 A.M. with my Dutch Bros. Iced Orange Groove Cold Brew in hand and find a seat at a table near the back door of the cafeteria with the CTE teachers. The Career Technical Education teachers are somehow more laid back than the other teachers I've met this year. And since I've met a total of 7 so far, that's saying a lot.

The teacher I sit next to is a tall, lanky man wearing thick glasses, a thick head of curly, black hair, and a wide smile. He reminds me of an un-bearded Bob Ross, but since my sister tells me Bob Ross wasn't always cool, I keep the compliment to myself.

"You must be new," he says cheerfully. He sits with nothing but a bottle of water in front of him, and I can't help but assume he must have already finished his Iced Orange Groove Cold Brew… I don't even want to imagine starting the day without any caffeine.

"How can you tell?" I ask a little shyly. This man is old enough to be my dad, and I suddenly realize that all my colleagues are older than me. Not just older—significantly older. As this epiphany is happening, the swarm of butterflies in my stomach become active again.

"Well, I don't recognize you, so I just assumed. I'm Robert. Welcome to Shipman."

I smile and shake the hand he has offered me.

We exchange small talk while I slurp down my delicious cold brew and watch the fluttering of people around me. I see several teachers hugging, and everyone has a giant smile on their faces. They all look genuinely happy.

I used to work the apparel department at one of the sporting goods stores nearby, and I never saw anyone *this happy* to be at work. In fact, I have never felt this happy to be at work either. This is the kind of stuff that makes me think I chose the right profession. Sure, all of these people here probably qualify for childcare and housing subsidies because of how little they get paid, but they're *happy*.

I overhear various conversations around me. A pod of teachers to my right discusses an Advanced Placement conference they attended. They enthuse over the speakers, complain about the food, and make plans to revise their syllabi together.

I want to revise my syllabi with someone. Actually, I want someone to teach me how to write a syllabus first, and then I want them to revise it with me.

Off to the left, I hear a group of *extremely* well-dressed teachers talk about fashion shows in New York and their Hawaii vacations. I wonder how they can afford such expensive trips as teachers, and make a mental note to investigate later. With two blue-collar parents, travel was never something I had an opportunity for. I am well aware that teaching may not ever afford me these types of opportunities in life either, so I am doubly intrigued to hear their conversation.

A loud screech tears through the happy chatter in the cafeteria, and my eyes immediately search for the source. I see the "tech guru," Mr. Wolf, trying to get the microphone connected to the giant speakers at the front of the cafeteria. A few more uncomfortable ring out, and I wonder how tech-savvy Mr. Wolf really is. In a moment, Mr. Sanders takes the microphone and steps onto the makeshift stage.

Mr. Sanders is a surprisingly short man. He looks to be about my height, 5'2, but I swear I can see over his head when we talk. I know because he has a remarkably shiny, bald head. Whenever I'm near him, I catch myself trying to find reflections in it. His flawless face is smooth except for a thin, black goatee, and his arms and calves are ridiculously muscular. He was obviously some sort of coach or bodybuilder in the past. Actually, maybe he still is. Do principals even have time to exercise?

He doesn't smile and doesn't have any warmth about him as he prepares to start the meeting. I glance at my watch that says 7:15 A.M. It's odd to me that the meeting is starting so late, especially given his specific instructions in his last minute email that all staff needed to be here at 7:00 A.M. *'sharp'*.

7:00 A.M. sharp, my tush.

"Ladies and gentlemen of Shipman high," his monotone voice begins, "it's my pleasure to welcome you to an all new school year."

The teachers and staff sitting around the cafeteria clap. I don't clap though, because I'm pretty sure he's lying. He doesn't look like he is finding pleasure in *anything* today.

"If you've been following the news over the last few months, then you know our very own Penelope Juarez has been leading the charge on some new bills that have been passed and policies that have been adopted by the district."

Penny stands up at her table and gives a quick wave to everyone. Nobody applauds or waves back, and she sits back down gracefully.

"As such," Mr. Sanders continues, "Penny will be leading the charge here on campus, as well, to help us figure out how to implement these new policies. Before you leave, make sure to grab one of the blue flyers next to the cafeteria entrance. It's a quick and dirty outline of the new policies. Each of you will meet with your grade level PLC's this week to flush them out in more detail, so keep an eye on your inbox for emails from your department chairs."

I hear murmurs around the room but can't tell if they're disappointed or approving. However, I can tell that all the people understood what PLC stands for, so I lean over to Robert.

"What's a PLC meeting?" I ask, slightly embarrassed that there are so many acronyms I still don't know.

"PLC: Professional Learning Community. It's just everyone in your subject matter grade level. You'll meet to plan and look at common assessments," Robert explains.

I nod to show I understand, then turn my attention back to the stage.

Penelope stands up and faces the crowd. With a booming voice for such a tiny person, she says, "And the whole world will be watching us. The district chose us to be a pilot school in implementing these policies this year, so all the other schools in our district will be watching to see how it goes. And districts around the nation will be looking at us as an example."

She is beaming with pride, and the clapping that erupts in the cafeteria suggests she has good reason to. From where I sit, my colleagues as a whole seem genuinely happy. Well, it's that or they're all just really happy about whatever they're discussing. Only about half the conversations stopped when Mr. Sanders started speaking, and no one seemed to mind.

There are pretty good odds that only half the cafeteria even heard her announcement.

"Have a great first day, everyone. Dismissed!" Mr. Sanders finishes.

I can't believe we had a staff meeting on the first day of school to give us a flyer about things we will discuss later. I've heard all the jokes about how *this could have been an email,* but I didn't expect to experience it on the first day of school. I look at my watch and see that students will be allowed on campus in a mere 5 minutes.

I savor the rest of my delicious Dutch Bros. indulgence before heading back to class. I know I won't be able to afford coffee again for at least the rest of the month until I get my first paycheck, so here I sit—sipping, savoring, and sleuthing.

I watch the other teachers pick up the flyer, eager to see their reactions. Most don't bother reading it right away. A few skim quickly and give little nods. Most notable to me is the fact that nobody seems shocked or upset.

I finish my coffee and drop it in the trash on my way to the ominous blue stack of papers. There are probably 3 times the amount needed for the staff present, and I wonder if they anticipated teachers 'losing' them. I pick one up for myself and read the following:

New Policies Effective Immediately

1. Any supplemental text (this includes articles, books, YouTube clips, etc.) must be documented in advance, reviewed by and voted on by your entire PLC prior to its use.

2. All lesson plans must be posted online for community approval two weeks in advance. Any supplemental texts used in these plans should have already been reviewed and approved by your PLC. This means your lessons cannot be done at the last minute. Plan accordingly.

3. Teachers may not discuss a student's mental health status with them or anyone else at any time. Refer them to their counselors immediately using the Google form.

4. Teachers may not discuss any matters of sexuality or gender identity with any student outside of identification purposes. Any transgender students should be reported on the Google form.

My head is swimming trying to anticipate the consequences of each of these new policies, but processing all this information this early in the morning proves to be a challenge.

The first thing that comes to my mind is the amount of time I would have to spend to curate supplemental resources in advance. It would be completely unimaginable. As a new teacher, I don't have some magical filing cabinet full of vetted resources to pull from. But the real issue is having things approved *prior* to the lesson plans being posted… two weeks *prior* to them being taught. I barely have my lesson plans done for this first week of school; I can't imagine having two weeks of lesson plans. In advance.

I imagine that several teachers, like myself, will end up using absolutely nothing supplemental for fear of reprimand or consequences. Not to mention that lesson plans and unit plans can be fluid. I may not know I really need a video to help explain commas tomorrow until I come across it tonight in my desperation to meet a need I just discovered my students have. This policy really, really bums me out.

I don't have any experience teaching yet, but I had some amazing mentors in college who told me teachers are never stagnant. *Good* teachers, that is. A good teacher is constantly trying to learn as much as they can about their students and adapt their lessons to meet those needs. But how will teachers do this with such strict constraints on their resources and the timing for procuring them?

The third item on the list makes my stomach drop. It makes me cringe. It makes me angry. *Teachers may not discuss a student's mental health status with them at any time. Refer them to their counselors immediately.*

This was the very reason I became a teacher. How do you teach the Common Core standards through discussing the human condition in literature and *not* discuss mental health?

The very thing that made me fall in love with literature was that it let me know I wasn't alone. No matter how lonely I felt, someone, somewhere has felt that way, too. Books gave me that insight. How can I share that same freedom with students if this gag order is in place?

And what about the students who have already talked to me? At least three different students that met me at the meet and greet did so for the purpose of calming their anxious children.

And the last policy—the one about sexual or gender identity—how does that even work?

Before I can brainstorm any more worst-case scenarios in my head, the first bell signaling the students' presence on campus rings. I pick up my belongings and head to my classroom.

8

I navigate the labyrinth of hallways and only go down two wrong ones before making it to my classroom. I stash my belongings in my teacher's desk and put Vitamin String Quartet on the classroom speakers.

I grabbed the seating chart binder I created over the weekend. Each class period has its own tabbed sections with a seating chart. Each seating chart has been printed and put in a sheet protector to use a dry erase marker for attendance and notes. I grab the purple post-it piles I prepped over the weekend and begin to place each one with a carefully written student name on its corresponding desk.

Each desk has a name in a matter of moments, and I'm ready to begin class. I make my way to my classroom door and prop it open with a doorstop. I stand awkwardly in my succulent dress with a naively optimistic smile and my hands clasped in front of me. The bell to head to class hasn't rung yet, but various students wander the hallways trying to locate their classes. I figure I can stand in the hallway and try to chat with students or flit around nervously in my room. Neither one is going to help me be less nervous starting class today.

My hallway has all the freshman teachers, but I seem to be the only newbie this year. I can tell by the fact that I am the *only* teacher standing in the hall to greet students this early.

I lean against the wall next to my open classroom door for a moment and try to calm my breathing. I see two students standing under the skylight across from my room. One of them points up; they both cover their mouths, laughing hysterically, and then walk away quickly. Curious, I walk over to the skylight and look up.

The skylight is a large square in the ceiling. The clear glass letting in the sun has a criss-cross pattern of metal bars in front of it, presumably to tamper down on student skylight escapes. Dangling from different spots in the skylight, blowing ever so gently with the building's air conditioning, are multiple tampons.

While I'm thrilled to see schools have gotten more progressive in the feminine hygiene products they offer students (growing up we were only offered pads; apparently tampons were akin to losing our virginity), I'm not quite sure this is the best method of distribution. I'm slightly appalled and wonder how long the tampons have been hanging there.

I have so many questions, I can hardly contain myself. Like, how did they get up there? Who decided that tampons hanging freely about is a good look for the skylight? Are they tied to the metal crossbars? Who in heaven's name has the fingers nimble enough to tie tiny tampon strings around metal bars 10 feet into the air?

I shake my head gently, as if doing so might shake loose these insane thoughts, and walk back to my classroom door. The bell finally rings and students flood the hallways.

The memory of my Safe Space poster hits me right at that moment, so I rush back inside my classroom and dig through the only filing cabinet drawer until I find the laminated cardstock and my staple gun. I promptly go into the hallway and notice a few students lined up outside my open door. I determinedly attach the poster at eye level next to my door, then step back to admire my handiwork.

A grin spreads across my face with pride until I hear a slightly gravely voice just behind me say, "Miss, that is *so* crooked."

"Jax! It's so good to see you!" I say with excitement. Their hair is fashioned into a very tall mohawk with glittery purple tips. Their white t-shirt is torn in multiple places and their black bra is showing through. Their skirt stops mid-thigh and I'm struck by how many dress code violations they managed to acquire in *one outfit*.

I have already decided I will not dresscode kids out of my own personal principles. I know it's the rules, but I can't dresscode kids. Also, I'm shorter than at least half of them and look younger than several. Who's going to care what I say about their clothing? On top of that, I wouldn't know *what* to say about their clothing. Who would I even report that to? Is there a report to fill out?

See? It's a bad idea all around.

I take another two steps away from the door to see if the poster is really that crooked, and it is. A few of the students waiting to enter the room walk over and help me adjust the poster until it's sufficiently straight for Jax's satisfaction.

"Okay, Miss. I guess I'm going to go to class now."

Jax's lack of enthusiasm is almost contagious, but I respond over-enthusiastically to try to make them smile. "Yay! You're going to have so much fun!" I shout. "I can't wait to see you later!" I wave with ridiculous vigor and give them a parting smile.

Finally finished, I turn and welcome students into the classroom. I say good morning to each person as they enter and instruct them to find their seat with their name on a post-it. Most students don't look at me or respond when I speak, but I continue smiling at each student.

I see a student with a giant marijuana leaf on his beanie and a Cheech and Chong picture on his black hoodie. He enters without acknowledging me, and I'm shocked that he's walking around in an outfit advertising marijuana.

My surprise doesn't last long, though. Another three students enter the room with names of dispensaries or famous potheads on their clothes. Most of the girls wear crop tops with their arms crossed in front of their tummies. I'm starting to think there are fewer students *following* the dress code than not. I wonder if I'll really get into trouble if administrators see students walking out of my classroom with dresscode violations. I'm starting to think I should make a list of questions I have about my job description and responsibilities.

Instead, I continue greeting students until the final bell rings. Once it does, I carefully bend down to retrieve the door stop, take a deep breath to steady myself, and hear a small *riiiiiiip* tear through the silence of the hallway. My face automatically heats up with shame. It's almost as if I don't even have to know where the rip came from—it's just fated to be embarrassing. I remain out of sight from the doorway and awkwardly check the seams of my dress.

On the left, right at my waist, is a very noticeable tear. "Nooooo," I moan as quietly as I can. I stomp my foot in protest to… myself, and notice—much to my chagrin—that at least I have the right day from my days-of-the-week underwear on. The word MONDAY is stamped all over my butt in various fonts.

"And that's how, on my first day of teaching, I learned *not* to wear days of the week underwear or freaking Etsy dresses with silly plants on them," I say to my imaginary biographer.

I put my hands on my hips to hide the tear and make my way to my desk as inconspicuously as possible. I check every empty drawer for what I know I won't find—a safety pin or *something* to keep my dress together. I frantically open and close each drawer twice, just to make sure. I'm cursing myself for not being more prepared. This isn't even the first time I've accidentally ripped a dress I was wearing. You'd think I'd manage to stock safety pins by now.

Thankfully, the students haven't seemed to notice

anything is amiss… or that they're in a classroom… Not a single person is looking up from their phones. I try to take a few deep breaths again and figure out what I'm going to do. My eyes fall on all the different items of my desk: my coveted and one and only flair pen that I could afford, the flyer from the meeting this morning, and… a stapler!

I gleefully grab the pink stapler and sit in my seat. I verify that the students are still in zombie cell phone mode, then I bunch up my dress and angle myself under my desk as much as possible. I quickly staple the fabric together twice, without worrying about damaging it. At this point, all I care about is that students know the day of the week because I wrote it on the board—not because it's written on my ass.

I look up nervously, hoping no one has noticed, and not a single student has lifted their heads from their cell phones or desks. I breathe a sigh of relief while tying my light green sweater around my waist. No need to show off my new look: *stapled-chic.*

I start class by introducing myself and my degree from Cal State Los Angeles. Then we play "Two Truths & a Lie". The object of the game is to guess which of the 3 statements made by a person are true. It allows students to get to know each other a little bit without too much social risk-taking.

"Alright, I'll go first. See if you guys can figure out which of these are lies. I have 7 siblings, I'm allergic to cats, and I could live off of Dutch Bros. coffee. Which one is false? Raise your hand if you think I'm lying about having 7 siblings!" Nobody raises their hand.

"Raise your hand if you think I'm lying about cat allergies!" Again, nobody raises their hand.

"Raise your hand if you think I'm lying about my coffee addiction!" I'm really trying to maintain enthusiasm for the activity, but nobody is raising their hands.

"Wow, guys. Am I to believe you *really* don't care about

my cat allergies and coffee addictions?" A few students crack a smile and one even chuckles a little. I repeat my two truths and lie and tell the students we will do it until everyone has voted. This gets immediate participation.

Students guess correctly that I don't have 7 siblings, then I give them 5 minutes to write out their own two truths and a lie. When the timer goes off, I eagerly take my spot at the front of the room again and ask for volunteers.

"Do I have any brave students who would be willing to go first?" I ask hopefully. A student near the back punches the air to volunteer. I check the seating chart before saying, "Fernando! Awesome! Tell us your two truths and your one lie."

He stands up and cracks his neck. He adjusts his Cheech and Chong sweatshirt before beginning. "Okay, I'm smart, I'm funny, and I'm not good at basketball."

Oh no.

Oh… no.

How am I going to keep this kid from getting bullied during his first ever class assignment? Who chooses subjective statements for two truths and a lie? Oh man, if I ask for students to vote on the lie, hands are going to go up when I ask if he's lying about being cool or funny, and I'm worried that's going to hurt. I'm also concerned for the rest of this kid's high school career. I figured middle school would have gotten rid of any remaining naivety, but I guess that's not the case for all my students.

"Okay…" I start to say. I have no idea how to handle this situation. All I know is that students can't vote on whether or not this kid is cool. "How about if we stick to facts that we can prove?"

"Miss!" Fernando shouts, legitimately shocked. "I *am* smart! That's a fact! And I'm funny. Fact."

"Oh! So your lie was that you're bad at basketball?" I ask innocently. I can feel the butterflies that were starting to get active calming down. I'm so relieved we've solved the mystery without having to have students vote on it.

"Yeah! I'll ball you up, Miss!"

"Okay, so you're smart, funny, and good at basketball. Thanks for sharing. Who's next?" My eyes search desperately for another willing participant before Fernando adds anything extra that might require me to shield him from ridicule.

A student in the front says, "I'll go!" He stands up and says, "Hey y'all. I'm Jordan. What's good? Okay here are my two truths and a lie: I once punched my mom in the face, I have a pet squirrel, and I'm a girl."

Oh. Shit.

Now we're guessing about gender? And punching people's mothers in the face? I swear to God, nothing in my teaching program could have prepared me for this. Why don't they warn you about what comes out of teenager's mouths? I'm not sure I could get any more uncomfortable, but I'm sure this is the last time I will ever play this game with high school students.

The rest of the day is significantly less eventful. Little, if anything, is taught or learned; it's a day for counting attendance, identifying scheduling errors, distributing electronic devices, and having students physically sign their name to a piece of paper 8 different times in one day to prove they really exist. And since I couldn't fill the small bouts of class time with my brilliant getting-to-know-you game, I try to use the time to get to know my students on a more personal level.

My favorite professor at my university gave us this amazing resource to get to know students during the first few weeks of school. On one side of the paper, there is a set of boxes labeled for the first two weeks of school. Each box has one spot for the student to leave a question, comment, or fun fact, and a corresponding box for the teacher's response. Students decorate the other side with their preferred name and pronouns. I've decided this *has to* go better than the Two Truths & a Lie game.

I pass out the paper to the students and say, "Go ahead and fold this into thirds like a hotdog, the long way." I stand in front of the class to model how to fold the triangular-shaped nameplate and watch the students in front of me while trying to project a false sense of the confidence I'm completely lacking. Somehow, having students proclaim they've punched their mothers and they'd like their classmates to guess their gender really takes the wind out of my sails.

I have 33 desks in my classroom, but 41 students in this class period. Three students sit on a long table meant for keeping student resources accessible, one student sits at my teacher desk, three students sit on the floor at the back of the room, and one student stands against the side of the room for the entire 55 minute period.

I watch students *seriously* struggle with folding their papers into thirds. Several students have folded it in half, and a few students haven't even picked up their papers. I walk around and try to encourage students to assist their group members before I return to my position at the front of the room.

Grabbing a marker from the caddy on the group of desks in front of me, I write on my demonstration paper, *Ms. White (she/her)* and hold it up.

I tell the students, "This is going to act like your nameplate for this first quarter. Each day, you will put it on your desk so that I can learn your names. At the end of each day, you will fill out one of the boxes inside for me to read and respond to.

"But for now, let's just focus on the nameplate. Use the markers and colored pencils in front of you to write your name *largely* and *clearly*," I try to emphasize. "Then, add some doodles or words and phrases around your name that describe you. On my nameplate, I might draw several cups of coffee, the Blink 182 logo, and maybe a longboard. Those are all things I love. Be as creative as you like. You have 30 minutes,"

I finish.

I wind the over-sized magnetic timer on my whiteboard and use the time to take attendance and collect signatures. Or at least, that was my plan. I thought that if I gave the kids time to doodle independently, that would give me time to confirm their identities.

The 30 minutes finishes faster than I can take attendance, and I realize only half of the students have even written their names on their nameplates. I decide to pause collecting signatures and inform the students they must put their name and a question or comment on the inside of their nameplates, and that I would be responding to every single one of them. I hear a few grumblings in addition to all the unfolding of papers and a few pens clicking.

Once I've finished taking attendance, I hardly have time to collect the nameplates before the bell rings and the students run off as quickly as they can. I'm proud that I survived a full class period, but disappointed at how little I got to interact with the students. The whole thing felt rushed and forced. I wonder if it will always be this hard.

9

By the time the last bell of the day rings, I'm in a complete daze. I somehow managed to keep moving through each class period, even though I felt like I didn't know what I was doing. Once the last student has left the room, I plop myself down unceremoniously on my pathetic blue desk chair and let out a massive sigh I'd been holding in all day. Glancing at my watch, I realize I only have a moment to rest because our first PLC meeting is starting soon.

My Professional Learning Community (or "PLC" because educators have a passion for acronyms) is made up of 3 other teachers teaching the same grade level and content. This first meeting of the year will take place in Giselle Hawkins's classroom, so I stand back up, grab a notepad and pen, and make my way to her room.

Giselle has been teaching English for the last decade. Her room is so meticulous that any student stepping foot inside would know the teacher has things under control. There are labeled bins for everything: work to turn in, work to pass back, writing utensils, coloring utensils, class sets of books, and anything else a student could possibly need.

Even more impressive is the wall behind her immaculate desk. It's covered in letters from students throughout the decade. I sneak a peek at a few of them to see what I can learn about Giselle.

Dear Ms. Hawkins,

Even though we don't really talk much, I very much appreciate the effort you put into teaching. Your awkward/funny sense of humor always makes me laugh and look forward to going to your class. BTW sorry I'm always late to your class (it's the stairs) but I enjoy how fun you make class. You make learning a fun experience and teach in a way that makes it easier. You show that you genuinely care for the safety & progress of each of your students. Making your students feel comfortable enough to talk to you about anything is a very much appreciated characteristic. I honestly enjoy going to your class because there's never a dull day and everything is always interesting. Anyways, I hope you get many more teacher appreciation letters because you deserve to be appreciated in great ways.

My heart warms, and an unexpected smile spreads across my face. It sounds like Ms. Hawkins might be the type of teacher Stacy needed—the kind of teacher I aspire to be. I read another letter on her wall that says,

Dear Y'all,

You are very lucky to have a teacher that is passionate about what they do. Some may not be used to happy teachers. I know I wasn't used to it, but it is an awesome thing in the end. Ms. Hawkins was there when I needed to talk, and it's not common for many teachers to do so, so take advantage of having an adult to open up to when you are at your worst. School seems hard now, but keep going, and school will get easier.

I'm immediately assured that Giselle is someone I definitely want to get to know and learn from. My eyes wander back to the notes and reread, "*Ms. Hawkins was there when I needed to talk"* and *"Making your students feel comfortable enough to talk about anything."*

As I'm about to start reading another letter, Giselle interrupts me when she reenters the room from setting up her doorstep.

"Feel free to take a seat anywhere," she says, gesturing to the room full of empty desks.

"Thanks," I say quietly. I guess there's no inconspicuous way to continue reading the letters behind her desk, so I turn to find a seat. Something about her makes me a little nervous. I think it's the admiration. Giselle is technically my peer, but with her experience and the respect she seems to have from her students, I have a lot to learn from her.

I make my way to a desk near the front of the room and set down my pen and notepad. Within moments, a few other teachers have entered the room and found their respective seats—all oddly far away from one another. Since they're all sitting behind me, I have no way to look at them without making it weird, so I stare down at my notepad and doodle.

After a few more moments, Penny finally enters by herself and walks straight to the podium at the front of the small room to start the meeting. Her facial expression says she is all business, and her short blond hair is fashioned into perfect, loose curls around her head as usual. Despite the grim facial expression she wears, the royal blue track jacket zipped up over a t-shirt and jeans she is also wearing make her seem less scary.

Penny starts the meeting by asking, "How was everyone's first day back?" Her voice is cordial enough, but her smile doesn't reach her eyes. She looks exhausted, but she's obviously trying to hide it. Without giving anyone time to answer her question, Penny continues, "I want to make sure everyone gets a chance to meet Samantha White, our new English 9 teacher. Let's start by introducing ourselves and what we all teach."

"I'm Giselle Hawkins, 9th grade English and AVID," our host begins. Giselle is about 5'7 with unruly blond, wavy hair. Her hair is pulled back into a loose ponytail, but stray pieces rebel all over the top of her head. She wears thin, blue, wiry glasses over her half-faded makeup. Even though it's the first day of school, Giselle wears comfortable jeans and a Shipman High polo. She looks casual but confident.

"AVID?" I ask, confused by another acronym. I'm starting to think I should be carrying around a tiny notebook everywhere I go to collect acronyms. How is it possible that no database of acronyms exists for teachers yet? How do teachers remember all of this?

"Advancement Via Individual Determination," she responds. "Basically, it's a class that helps students learn important study skills to get them to college. It's a class for the 'bubble kids'—kids who are on the cusp of success but just need a little push."

My interest is definitely piqued, and I make a mental note to find out more about AVID later on. I nod my head to convey I'm following along, and the next person speaks.

"Yeah, Diogo Kaufman here," says a rather tall, sculpted man. He wears a deep blue button-up paisley shirt and khaki pants. On top of his head is the silkiest, dark brown hair I have ever seen in my life. It has a slight curl to it and looks like the kind of perfect hair that models in surfing commercials always seem to possess.

I can just imagine him walking out of the ocean in a wet suit, with the tight neoprene clinging to his well-defined arms as he carries his surfboard out of the water. Just as the imaginary Diogo in my head is about to slowly and dramatically shake the salt water out of his hair, my reverie is interrupted.

"I teach 9th-grade honors, and 9th-grade honors accelerated."

I wonder what the difference is between an honors class and an honors accelerated class, but keep my question to myself. At least it gives me something to wonder about other than how Mr. Kaufman's perfect hair would feel between my fingers…

"You all know me, your department chair, Penny Juarez," the voice from the front of the room says. "I'm teaching English 9, I have two sections of co-taught English this year, and I'm also the cheer coach." That explains the track jacket, but shouldn't the cheer coach seem more… cheerful?

At last, all eyes fall on the teacher sitting next to me. She's at least six feet tall with perfectly straight, brown hair, perfectly shaped eyebrows amid her flawless face, and the tallest pink high heels I have ever seen a teacher wear. She doesn't any makeup, and she's easily one of the most beautiful women I've ever seen.

"Emma Holland, English 9, English 9 honors, and I'm also the girl's basketball coach."

"How's the team looking this year, Holland?" Diogo asks, and it's only now that I notice his emerald green eyes. They're a bright contrast to his dark skin and sparkle like *"a rich jewel in an Ethiope's ears."* His eyebrows are like two brown, fuzzy caterpillars wearing parkas in the winter, but I can overlook that.

Oh my god. I'm losing it.

I shake my head to try to redirect my thoughts.

Penny remains standing at the podium with her all-business expression. "Alright, now that we've all met each other, I have everything you need to know about the new policies and how we're going to implement them."

I ready my pen and prepare to take notes, as I'm sure there's a lot to keep track of. I really, *really* don't want to upset any parents or administrators during my first year of teaching. With my anxiety as bad as it is, I'm not sure I'd recover… I guess that's another one for the "Reasons Dad Was Right About My Career" column.

"First things first, in our shared Google Drive, there is a file called *Supplemental Texts*. Any video clips, articles, comics, memes, podcasts, etc. that aren't provided by the school *must* be on this form at least three weeks in advance."

"Three weeks?" Emma asks with shock.

"Yeah, three weeks," Penny confirms. "This gives us a week to review the material and approve it while you write your lesson plans with the approved resources, and then two weeks to have the lesson published online for parent feedback. This means we will need your lesson plans for the rest of this month posted online by the end of this week."

I'm hoping my eyes aren't actually bugging out of my head the way they feel they are because it's probably not the most professional look. It's also not the best way to inspire my colleagues' confidence in me. I make a respectable effort to compose my face and jot down on the notepad I brought: *ALL LESSONS DUE FRIDAY*. I make a point to write in all capital letters, so I don't forget the importance of this.

Penny continues to inform us, "It also means you need to have all supplemental items added to the file in the Google Drive this week as well."

I try not to freak out. How am I going to get an entire month's worth of lesson plans written during my *first week* of school? How am I supposed to manage this?

Emma stops Penny and asks, "What about the materials we used last year? Can we assume those are all approved?"

"Due to the sheer number of Pixar films being shown instead of actual classwork, it is definitely *not* safe to assume materials from last year are acceptable this year," Penny responds matter-of-factly.

I hear Giselle scoff and say, "What about the texts we used last year? Not videos—but actual articles? Can we use those?"

"It all has to get approved, Ms. Hawkins."

"Can't we all just agree right now to approve all the articles we used last year?" Ms. Holland asks.

Penny's face reddens slightly, and a tight smile crosses her face. I can tell she wasn't expecting these kinds of questions when she rolled out the new policies for us. She uses Ms.

Holland's question to segue into how the community and parent approval process works.

"So parents get to decide what we teach?" Ms. Holland clarifies.

"It's really not about parents deciding what gets taught," she tries to explain, "it's about parents having access to the actual sources and materials being used in the classroom, so parents can have a more honest dialogue about what's happening at school."

"Well, why not approve all the materials from last year? We know they're rigorous and purposeful since we selected them, and we can provide parents with all the articles now. In advance." Emma makes a good point. Penny looks irritated with Emma's constant questions and suggestions.

"Emma, everything is going to go through the same process, alright? This is the district's policy so that we will follow it."

Emma rolls her eyes and tilts her head down as she does so, as if to hide it from Penny. Emma doesn't seem like the type of person to passive-aggressively roll her eyes, though, so maybe she didn't care if Penny saw her.

It sounds like Penny is trying to convince everyone this new policy is a positive thing. I'm trying hard not to have an opinion on whether it's a good thing or a bad thing. As I've been reminded multiple times, new teachers need to keep their heads down if they want tenure and continued employment. And as for me, well... I really like having a paycheck. I mean, I haven't exactly had one *yet*, but I'm really anticipating it to be a thrilling event.

"You can also find a Google form to fill out if students attempt to confide in you about anything related to mental health or gender identity. Neither of those topics is academic, so they shouldn't be happening in the classroom. If a student attempts to discuss either with you, let them know you'll fill out one of these forms and shut down the conversation."

My heart starts racing. Adrenaline is coursing through my

veins. My chest seems to be tightening, and I'm not sure why I'm about to have a panic attack. I reach into my pocket and pull out the tiny secret Xanax pill I keep in a little container on my key chain. I don't have any water, but I'm all-too-familiar with the bitter, stinging taste that comes with chewing a Xanax. I pop the tiny oval in my mouth and get to chewing as discretely as possible. Why aren't Xanax mints a thing yet?

I glance around the room at the other teachers to gauge their reactions to the information Penny is disseminating. Giselle sits at her personal desk on her computer in the back of the room. Her eyes never glance up from her computer screen, so I can't tell if she's even processing this information right now. If she is, she doesn't seem the least bit concerned.

With his perfect, wavy dark brown hair, Diogo is jotting down notes around a doodle of a mandala on his own notepad. His face doesn't look concerned either. With the perfect, silky smooth skin on his face, he doesn't look like he's ever been concerned about anything. He must be close to 30, but his face could easily pass for 21—especially given his lack of facial hair. I wonder how long he's been teaching and how many policy changes he has seen in his career. Regardless, his face is flawless, and hard to tear my eyes away from.

Emma hasn't looked up from her cell phone since Penny started talking, but she seems to be smirking a lot. I'm assuming her focus isn't entirely on this meeting because I haven't found anything to smirk about so far.

Diogo's hand goes up slightly as if he were a student himself. As if someone so tall and perfect looking could ever be mistaken for a student. Penny calls on him, and he asks, "So, what do we do if a student says, 'hey, I want to kill myself?' Do we really just say, 'Sorry, I can't talk about that, but let me fill out this form, and someone will hopefully get back to you in 4-6 weeks?'"

I hear Emma stifle a snicker, but she still hasn't looked up from her screen, so I can't definitively determine the source of said snicker.

Penny shakes her perfect blond curls in preparation for her response, and I can't help but wonder if perfect hair is an unspoken requirement for teaching here. Or if everyone just goes to the same salon…

"No, no," Penny assures him. "If a student is in immediate danger or is a danger to themselves, we're still mandated reporters. You have a legal obligation to immediately report that to the counselors or social workers. But it is *not* your job to get involved."

"What if a student comes to us specifically and isn't comfortable talking to their counselor?" Giselle asks. The question seems to be important enough to her that she's stopped working on whatever she was doing at her desk.

"Admin wants teachers away from anything remotely related to what our counselors and social workers do," Penny explains.

Emma finally looks up from her cell phone, still with a slight smirk. She clears her throat as if to clear the smirk and asks, entirely seriously, "So when our two counselors are busy with the other 500 kids on their caseload and our one social worker has a line of 5 kids outside her door to do suicide protocols with, what do we tell our one student who is an immediate danger to themselves?"

"Just call campus security, okay Holland? It's no longer your concern or your worry."

"Well, if it's my student, it *is* my concern," Emma retorts.

"You, of all teachers, should be relieved. Wasn't this one of your main complaints last year? Teachers having to act like social workers and counselors—things we were never trained for? Well, now Shipman High has solved that problem. Teachers will *only* discuss academics with students."

"Way to take it from one extreme to the next. Either teachers do *everything*, or they aren't allowed to do *anything*," I hear Giselle say from her desk.

Emma doesn't even try to hide her eye roll this time. She lets her eyes fall back to her phone and seems to tune out again.

My stomach is in knots, and I have the intense urge to get away from here as quickly as possible. I try my 4-7-8 breathing while attempting to listen to the continued conversation. Diogo asks for the counselors' extensions for emergencies, and then the topic seems to die down.

Giselle asks questions about copies, and Penny responds with a smile that doesn't seem even slightly genuine. "I'm so glad you asked! So this year we don't have *any* paper for *any* teachers. There are two incredibly old copiers in the teacher's lounge that you may use with your own paper, but admin has said they won't be servicing them. Once it's dead, it's dead."

"So, how are we supposed to make copies?" Emma asks. Emma and her logical questions.

"You're not. Every kid was issued a Chromebook during the pandemic. We know kids are capable of digital learning. We lived through it. There's no excuse for going back to paper. We just don't have the funds," Penny concludes.

Several moments pass without anyone saying anything. I try to look around the room at my colleagues inconspicuously, but it doesn't matter. Not a single one of them is looking up.

"That means," Penny adds, "if the copier gets jammed, we fix it ourselves, or it's out of use for good."

The Xanax I chewed is starting to kick in, thankfully. I can feel my entire body relaxing into an almost heavy-feeling slouch. My thoughts have stopped racing, and I can focus on the conversation at hand rather than running through the what-ifs in my head.

What if Stacy had asked a teacher for help? What if Stacy's teacher had told her they couldn't discuss the matter with her, but they'd fill out a Google form? What if she had plans for her suicide and asked for help without indicating immediate danger, but her teacher said, 'Sorry, I can't discuss this with you; wait for your counselor.' What if Stacy was going to ask for help, thought she didn't matter after being referred to a Google Form, then went home and ended her life?

I honestly don't know how reasonable my fear and anxiety about student suicides are and how much of it is just PTSD from Stacy. Either way, I'm so glad the Xanax has started working its magic, and I can now focus on the fact that I will be buying my own paper and making my own copies for the rest of my career.

Penny reminds us of a few upcoming deadlines for finishing the mandatory online district trainings, lesson plan submission deadlines, and the forthcoming Welcome Back Staff Luncheon that will be held on Friday in the teacher's lounge.

Once she dismisses everyone, the other teachers quickly grab their belongings and leave the room. Not one of them lingers to chat, which I find disappointing. Not only was I hoping to ogle Kaufman's hair some more, but I was also actually hoping to talk to my new colleagues. Instead, they all raced out quickly.

Except for Giselle, who continues to sit at her desk, unperturbed. Her fingers continue to type away frantically, giving the impression that she's completely absorbed with her task at hand. She never looks up at Penny after the meeting ends. Penny finishes gathering her belongings and walks out without saying goodbye to either Giselle or myself.

Once she's gone, I summon all the energy from any secret reserves I might have and pull my heavy body out of the desk I'm sitting in. I'm grateful when my Xanax stops my panic attacks, but the pill's effects last significantly longer than the event itself. I try to avoid taking it unless I feel the situation I'm going into is unavoidable. I think I'm noticing a pattern here…

As I slowly walk out of Giselle's room, she says, "Hey Samantha, let me know if you ever need anything. I'm not super social, but I am a good sounding board, and I'll try to help with anything I can."

Her smile seems genuine, and the letters from her past students seem even more so. I give her a polite nod and leave to get the rest of my belongings. I don't think I can leave campus quickly enough today.

10

That evening, I sit cross-legged on my bed, reruns of the show *Ted Lasso* playing in the background, reading through the questions and comments on the students' nameplates. It takes me about 20 minutes to realize the process will go faster if I unfold each of the nameplates first. I know I have about a 180 to go through, and I'm really, really glad we only have all eight classes once this week. Tomorrow is an even day, so I focus on nameplates from my even class periods.

I grab my favorite (and only) Flair pen and begin reading and responding.

I don't have any questions.
    -Great! Let me know if you do!

My pronouns are they/them.
    -Thanks for the info! My pronouns are she/her.

I'm not gay.
    -Okay! Thank you for the information… I definitely will not ever ask you about your sexual orientation.

I look at the last student's comment. He's not gay? Why would he think I would... ask for that information? I understand students coming out, but I didn't think that extended to straight kids. I'm wondering if it's because the paper asked for his preferred pronouns. I make a mental note to speak to the student the next time I see him.

I check the top and see his name is Oliver Park. Oliver is in my first period, so I'll have to wait until Wednesday to see him. I put a yellow post-it on his paper to remind me when I pass them back. I also take a moment to double check the stack I'm grading and realize I have been working on the stack from my Wednesday classes instead of tomorrow's.

Although they all have to get read and responded to at some point, I'm frustrated with myself for not realizing my mistake sooner. I know I will have to spend a ridiculous amount of time on my lesson plans this weekend, so I'm trying to get my grading done during the week.

Unfortunately, when I excitedly gave out this assignment, I didn't consider the fact that there was only *one* of me and 180 of *them!*

I switch the stack on my lap for the one on my nightstand and keep reading.

Who is my counselor?

-Great question! Your counselor is Ms. Nguyen. You can find her email address on the school website!

Why are you so energetic?

-Probably all the coffee. My family once tried to do an intervention...

I'm really nervous about making friends.

-You're not alone! The real secret is that every person is just as nervous as you are! Be bold! Be brave!

Say hello to someone new! You're going to have a great year!

Why did you ask for our pronouns?

-So I can respectfully use the correct pronouns when referring to you!

As I finish the last few nameplates for tomorrow, I realize there's a trend. Several students seemed confused about pronouns. One student at least *asked* what the deal was with them, but another student thought I was asking if they were gay. I'm starting to feel like I might be getting in over my head.

I stuff the finished stack of papers into my teaching bag and start getting ready for bed. I realize I will have to address this with my students tomorrow, and I have no idea what to say.

Well, at least I'll have something to obsess about while I lay awake tonight…

It took me a full 24 hours to decide how to address the pronoun confusion with my students. I've decided to handle it on a case-by-case basis because I think most students understand why I have asked their pronouns and understand the definition of the word *pronoun*.

On Wednesday morning, I make sure to take my Xanax before the first bell of the day rings. I know I will need all my calm and professionalism when talking to Oliver, who is only a handful of years younger than me.

Once class has begun and the students are seated, I pass back the nameplates and ask them to please set them up to display their names. I pull the post-it off Oliver's paper before returning it to him and ask if I can speak with him outside.

Oliver is about my height but seems much taller with his curly hair. He makes no facial expressions whatsoever when I ask to speak with him, but he silently stands up and walks towards the door. I grab his nameplate off his desk and follow him into the hallway. The door closes behind us, and I take a step away from him.

"Hey Oliver," I begin somewhat nervously. I feel my Xanax from earlier starting to kick in, so I have more confidence in my ability to handle this professionally. "I noticed you wrote that you're not gay on the spot that asked for your pronouns next to your name."

"That's 'cause I ain't!" He growls.

I'm shocked that he's so angry, but at least my adrenaline isn't pumping, so I can think a little more clearly. I say 'little' because the Xanax slows me down significantly. Sometimes I feel like it makes me dumber.

"Okay, well, first, I wanted to make sure you know that I will never ask you if you're gay or straight. That is not my business."

"Then why'd you ask me for my pronouns?"

Thanks to the medicinal aide, I do my very best to remain patient, and I'm remarkably successful. "Would you be upset if I called you 'she' or 'her'?" I ask.

"I ain't no girl!" Again, he seems considerably agitated.

"Okay," I continue calmly, "so you prefer the pronouns 'he' and 'him.'"

"But I ain't gay!" he insists again.

Feeling my frustration breaking through the barrier of the Xanax calm, I say, "Oliver, I really don't care if you're gay or not—"

"I ain't gay!" he shouts again.

I realize I'm drowning here and try again. "I just needed to know if you would like to be referred to as 'he' and 'him.' If that sounds good, we can go back inside."

"Yeah, I'm a boy," he says, his anger dissipating slightly.

I nod my head in understanding while painfully concealing my inner frustration, then pull the door open for Oliver to return to his seat.

I take a deep breath, then follow him into the room.

I pull a copy of Six-Word Memoirs off the tidy shelf next to my desk for today's class. Like everything on this shelf, it is my own personal copy that I've marked up and responded to. The paperback cover is worn and bent; the pages automatically open up to a few sections that have been read ceaselessly. This particular copy, *A Terrible, Horrible, No Good Year: Hundreds of Stories on the Pandemic* is a recent publication that most students can relate to.

During the COVID-19 pandemic, everything we knew about education was put to the test. Districts struggled to figure out how to deliver quality education to socially distanced students from diverse backgrounds with widely varying resources and means. When the pandemic hit, I was in my first year of college, and the world shut down completely to quarantine.

After completing my Intro to Teaching Seminar, this Six-Word Memoirs book was one of my first purchases. I knew that the students I'd be teaching shortly would be different from generations prior, and I hoped this book might be a way to bridge the gap between my understanding and their need for connection with a caring adult. And, as an added bonus, I've seen lots of teachers on Facebook talking about doing Six-Word Memoirs with their classes, and it's always a big hit.

"Does anyone know what the word 'memoir' means?" I ask casually while flipping through my book. I've heard that students are more likely to respond to casual-conversational questions about academic topics—and the last thing I want is to talk to myself all day. But it looks like that's exactly what I'm getting. I take a deep breath.

"Has anyone ever heard the word *memoir* before?" I try again. I raise my eyebrows and make a slightly silly, curiously confused face to try to create a safe and welcoming atmosphere.

Students rarely seem to volunteer an answer to a question

unless they *know* the answer is correct. It's as if the learning process has to happen entirely privately within one's own mind, or they're accused of not being as "smart" as other kids. My theory is that if I can lower their affective filters, I'll have more participation and student growth later on. Okay, it's not *my* theory; I just can't remember which of the dozens of educational theorists came up with it.

I write the word MEMOIR on the board in big capital letters and say, "Some of the most interesting books I've read are memoirs!" My over-the-top enthusiasm doesn't waver, and I hope I can keep the students interested. Under the word "MEMOIR," I carelessly write a quick list on the board:

- Anne Frank: The Diary of a Young Girl
- I am Malala
- Becoming (Michelle Obama)
- Orange Is the New Black
- A Long Way Gone: Memoirs of a Boy Soldier

Turning back to the class, I ask, "Can anyone find something these books have in common?" The students stare at the board. One or two heads cock to the side slightly, but most of them appear entirely lost. I want to give an awkward amount of wait time, hoping someone responds. I remember professors drilling into us the importance of waiting out our students. If we're brave enough to do it, they will respond.

But it's been a good 30 seconds, and I'm not sure I can handle the awkwardness, so I circle the first two letters of the word 'MEMOIR.'

"Ooh!" I hear someone shout, and a hand shoots up just as excitedly. I nod towards the student, and he responds, "They're about people."

"Yes!" I reply happily. Now, I feel like a real teacher, and I can feel the dopamine making me even more excited.

"Memoirs are stories about people and their experiences. How is that different from a biography?" I'm starting to *really* feel like a teacher now.

"Don't strangers write biographies?" a student asks.

"Yes!" I can't contain my excitement now. "That's exactly what is different between a memoir and a biography. If you ever forget, just look at the first two letters. Memoirs are written by and about *ME*." A few students slightly nod, and I'm noticeably more excited than the rest of them.

I explain that they will write a six-word memoir to introduce themselves to the class. But first, I read a few of the memoirs in the book I'm holding. These ones are specific to the COVID-19 pandemic experience for students and teachers, and the students seem to enjoy them. A few conversations are sparked about how masking felt as a kid, what distance learning looked like for them, and what the transition back to traditional in-person learning was like.

"See!" I begin excitedly, "You guys have *so* much to say! And what you have to say is important! Let's try a simple one. Think about this first week of school. Tell me everything I need to know about what this first week has been like *for you* — in exactly six words."

I instruct the students to take out a piece of scratch paper and jot down a few ideas while the ten-minute timer runs down. Once it goes off, I share mine out loud with the students, "First days still make me nervous." A few heads nod in agreement.

At least half the class has volunteered to share their six-word memoirs within minutes.

A girl says, "Finally a reason to cheer again." She's in a navy and baby blue track jacket that all the cheerleaders seem to wear. I wonder if it's the start of school or actual cheer events that she's referring to, and I decide to pretend she's referring to the first time she entered my classroom.

Another student stands up to say, "These J's look so damn fly," getting little murmurs of agreement in the back.

I smile and thank him for sharing before adding, "Don't say 'damn' in class."

The student's eyes go wide, and he says with vigor, "Ooh! Ms. White just swore in class!"

As if they'd been rehearsing this moment all morning, the rest of the class modulates their voice in a theatrical and in-sync, "Ooooh!"

My face begins to burn red-hot, and I feel my adrenaline pumping. I was not prepared for swearing in class today. Of all the scenarios I played out in my head, this wasn't one of them. I can't decide if this is worse than the kid saying he punched his mom in the face during our getting-to-know-you activities on the first day of school.

I pretended I didn't hear the students and passed out the assignment instructions to redirect their attention. I give them the rest of the period to create their own six-word memoirs while I circulate the room.

Every class period seems to enjoy the six-word memoir activity, and a few even collaborate on their memoirs. In my last class of the day, my honor's English class, I get a chance to see the ever cheerful Marie.

While standing at the door greeting students during the passing period, I see several of my students from other periods wave or make eye contact with me. I smile and wave at each one, relishing the feeling of being a teacher that *notices* students. I say hello to each of my current students as they walk in, though so few of them acknowledge me.

I see Marie in the hallway a few feet away, laughing and messing around with a group of three other girls. They're huddled around their phones, taking selfies and practicing TikTok dances. I glance at my watch and see that there are two minutes left in the passing period and wonder if any of those girls plan on attending class.

The bell finally rings, and I wait a moment before closing my door, hoping Marie will come to class at this moment, but none of the girls move. They continue giggling and staring at their phones. I decide I'm not familiar enough with the discipline policies to get involved with this, so I close my classroom door and begin class.

When I ask for volunteers to share their six-word memoirs, a shocking number of hands shoot up to volunteer.

Zero. Zero hands shoot up excitedly to share their memoirs. And I'm shocked.

With the amount of writing and discussion I saw during the last class session, I'm surprised so few are willing to share now.

"Alright, I guess I can't expect my students to do something I haven't at least done myself," I say. I write my own six-word memoir on the board for the class to see: *Oh snap, I'm a teacher now!* A few students giggle, and a hand shoots up quickly. I'm excited to see someone participate voluntarily, and I glance at the name on their nameplate. "Cody!" I proclaim joyfully.

"How long have you been teaching?" He asks, completely blindsiding me. I hoped that I could connect with the students by trying something new and being a beginner… but it hadn't occurred to me that they might ask how long I've been teaching. How is it possible that with all the ruminating and catastrophizing my brain does, students still manage to surprise me?

"Well, when I was a baby, I taught my parents how to survive with absolutely zero sleep or patience, so I'd have to say I've been teaching my whole life in one way or another."

I get a little chuckle from another student, but Cody seems unsatisfied. "Yeah, but like… how long have you been an actual *teacher* teacher?"

I shift my weight from one foot to the other while contemplating my response. A few ideas bump around in my head, but I really only have two options: lie or be honest. I want to lie and say I've been teaching five years, so they'll respect me or at least listen to me, but I also really want them to know that it's okay to be new and it's okay to mess up. It's all part of the process.

I count backward from 10 to steady my breathing before saying, "You know what, Cody? This is actually my *first* year teaching! Isn't that crazy? Just like it's your first year of high school, it's sort of *my* first week of high school, too. We all get to stumble through this year together and figure it out *together*. I promise not to be too hard on you if you promise not to be too hard on me. Deal?" I ask hopefully.

He doesn't respond for a minute, just pushes his glasses up on his nose. Like many of the students, he's wearing a black hoodie and jeans and sits at his desk, resting on his elbows. He seems to be thinking really hard about the proposition. His head cocks to the side for a moment.

Every student in the class is staring at him—as if his response will dictate theirs for the rest of the year.

"That's actually pretty cool, Miss," he says finally. I can feel my body relax beyond what my Xanax could have done for me at this moment, and I feel genuine joy and... love for this kid. The dopamine hits keep coming as I call the class back to the task at hand and ask again for some volunteers. Still, few seem willing to participate until a student asks, "Do we have to read our *own* memoirs?"

"That's a great idea! Let's do this. In your groups, share your memoirs with each other. Then, pick two to share with the whole class. Anyone in the group can read them, and you will still get to know your classmates a bit!" I'm delighted that a student made a suggestion, and I'm even more delighted that I was able to shift and adapt the activity. This is cloud nine.

I set the timer for 20 minutes and watched the groups awkwardly introduce themselves and decide who would share first. It's almost painful to watch how awkward it is for some students. I wish I could do something to make it less awkward, but that's just what happens during the first week of school. Everything is awkward and uncomfortable.

By the end of the class period, several memoirs are shared

and cheered for.

"Tomorrow will come; I'll keep going."

"Got shoe game. Everyone is jealous."

"I really hate all school work."

By the end of the 20 minutes, the students seem to be chatting more comfortably and naturally. I feel like the assignment was a tremendous success. Not wanting to stop the bonding, I collect everyone's assignments and allow them to continue socializing for the last few minutes of class.

As the week finally winds down, I reflect on some of the students I've started to get to know by name. Cody is the student who helped me save face in front of the students when I admitted to being a first-year teacher. He seems incredibly chatty and outgoing when he's in his group, so it feels like a major win getting him on my side this early on. I plan to love-on the challenging kids the most. Hopefully, with any luck, it will soften them into… *less* challenging kids… I guess.

Marie is the student whose mom seemed displeased that she's in an honors class. As if this wasn't already an indicator of a rough year to come, Marie hasn't greeted me once when entering class. She deliberately ignores me when I say hello and talks the entire time I'm talking during class. She ditched my class at least once this week, and today in class, she made snide remarks while kids were sharing their memoirs. Towards the middle of the period, she asked to go to the bathroom and never returned. I'm not really sure what to do with her.

And then there's Jax. I haven't seen Jax since the first day of school, and I'm a little worried. I know they mentioned having anxiety and school being one of their least favorite things, and I wonder what I might do to make it easier.

I decide at that moment that I'm going to use Google Voice or Remind to text any students on my roster that I haven't seen this week. I also decided this would probably be a good time to send a few other parents a welcome text. Once all the students have left class for the day, I take a seat at my desk and pull out my cell phone. I pull up our attendance program and check for students I haven't seen.

I hear a slight tapping on the door frame and look up from the attendance data to see Jax standing in the doorway.

"Jax!" I say happily, standing up to greet the student.

Jax's hair is brushed all to one side like when we first met, and they ditched the skirt. Today, Jax is wearing baggy jeans that are so ripped, I'm not sure what is the point of the pants. The shirt is their trademark white t-shirt with the black bra showing through. I wonder how they haven't been dress-coded yet.

Jax walks to my desk and hands me a folded piece of paper.

"It's my nameplate from Monday. I didn't get a chance to hand it in before class ended."

"Oh, thank you for bringing it to me. How has your week been?" I take the folded paper and put it on the pile of responses I plan to work through this weekend.

"Bad. I got in trouble for dress code."

My eyebrows shoot up, and I give them a look that hopefully conveys, *and you're surprised?*

"I know, but it's not okay. I should be able to wear whatever I'm comfortable in. I'm not a sex object, and it's not okay that the reason I can't wear what I want is that it might distract males... and make them think of sex? It's not okay."

I take a deep breath and hate that I agree so completely with Jax. The dress codes are archaic, and telling a student that two inches of their midriff showing is too immodest for school because it might distract and sexually arouse males is akin to blaming a rape victim for their clothing choices. I agree with Jax; it's not okay. But I don't know what to do about it.

"Jax, that sucks. I'm really sorry. That's really unfair."

"It's such bullshit," they say. Realizing what just came out of their mouth, they quickly add, "Sorry—I mean, this is crap."

A thin smile crosses my lips, but I try to keep it contained.

"Anyway, I just wanted to give you this paper. See you next week."

"Bye, Jax. Have a good weekend."

11

Saturday morning, I awake much too early for the Saturday after the first week of school. I would love to sleep in today, but I have a really cool opportunity this morning. The American Civil Liberties Union, or ACLU, advertised a virtual town hall to discuss students' right to learn and all the bills targeting transgender students. I signed up for it the moment I saw the advertisement.

Ever since Shipman became the pilot school for the type of policies the ACLU works to protect kids from, I have been searching for some way to help. As a first-year teacher, I know my hands are tied in many ways. There's so much I can't do or say without losing my job. And although many of these things might be issues I really would be willing to lose my job over, being out of the classroom isn't going to necessarily help students stuck inside classrooms. So, I keep my head down, my mouth shut, my eyes open, and I attend virtual town halls sponsored by the ACLU.

My biggest concern is Jax. I know they already have a lot of anxiety about going to school. The fact that they're nonbinary is a heavy weight to add to the already heavy burden of freshman year of high school.

Suddenly, I imagine an animated Jax performing the song "Under Pressure" from Disney's *Encanto*, and I can really see Jax relating to Luisa.

I once saw this incredible miniseries about a trans student's first year of secondary school. The series, First Day, chronicles the bullying, self-doubt, and dating woes of a typical teen—particularly as this trans teen experiences them. It gives me hope that there will always be good humans despite each new law or bill introduced.

I honestly don't know what I'm hoping to get out of this virtual town hall. Still, I would like to understand my actual limitations regarding discussing gender identity and sexual orientation, particularly regarding the literature we might read. Are we allowed to read stories with gay characters like *Simon Vs. The Homo Sapien's Agenda* or *The Perks of Being a Wallflower*? Are we allowed to discuss the Jenner family? Celebrity Tweets were all the rage for teaching grammar when I was in school—do we just make sure to omit celebrities like Neil Patrick Harris or Erin Page? Does pretending the LGBTQ+ community doesn't exist really benefit *anyone*? I do realize it would be easier for the majority if I didn't discuss anything remotely controversial, but the existence of people shouldn't be controversial.

Alright, I guess I *do* know what I'm hoping to get out of the virtual town hall.

Once I've gathered my phone, a cozy blanket, and another cup of coffee, I make myself comfortable in the armchair next to my bed. Logging into the live YouTube event is easier and more frustrating than expected. I really need to get a device with a bigger screen for this kind of stuff. My to-buy list keeps getting longer and longer.

#

The virtual town hall is a discussion between the ACLU Deputy Director of Transgender Justice and the ACLU's Senior Staff Attorney for their Speech, Privacy, and Technology

Project.

The moderator starts by acknowledging that current lawmakers really are targeting transgender people, emphasizing transgender youth overall. There are currently over 200 anti-LGBTQ+ bills across 35 states. These bills prevent healthcare for trans youth, prevent trans youth from participating in sports, and even threaten to investigate parents of trans youth for child abuse. This last part sounds shockingly similar to Shipman's new policies.

The number of anti-LGBTQ+ bills floors me. I had heard of a few over the last few years, but the news and media don't seem to give it much attention anymore, considering the sheer number of anti-LGBTQ+ bills. I immediately think about my students, and Jax in particular. What if Jax was denied healthcare, denied participation in school sports, or their parents were investigated for child abuse? What if this amazing mom—who made sure her children's teachers *knew* her child's correct pronouns—what if *she* were accused of child abuse for accepting her child?

It's hard to get out of my head and stop thinking about how this might affect my students, but I try to focus on the discussion.

The Deputy Director of Transgender Justice explains several different bills introduced around the country, including a Texas bill that would remove transgender children from their parents and place them in foster homes. He also mentions that most of the bills seem to really want to prevent gender-affirming care for trans youth, despite the fact that every major medical association agrees that this gender-affirming care significantly reduces the rate of suicide among transgender youth.

Stacy's face flashes into my mind. I'm suddenly 12 years old again.

I'm standing next to Stacy in front of a mirror at the store

Justice. We're trying on outfits for fun, and I convinced Stacy to try on a dress. I've never seen her in a dress. She typically wore skin-tight plaid pants, a blank t-shirt matching whatever color her pants were, no less than three different studded belts, and a pair of beat-up old Chucks. But now, she stood in front of the tall mirror outside her dressing room, staring at herself in a white dress covered in tiny pink flowers. Her puffy, curly hair looked out of place with such a pristine dress.

"You look beautiful!" I told her enthusiastically and honestly. That seemed to have been the wrong thing to say because her face reddened immediately, and she didn't look pleased. Still, she kept staring at herself in the mirror. Her eyes never left her image.

"Are you okay, Stacy?"

"My mom would probably cry of joy if I wore this dress," she said softly. Her thoughts weren't here shopping with us. They're somewhere else entirely.

"Who cares?" I said casually. "Wear whatever you like. Be yourself."

Those must have been the magic words to break her trance because she quickly looked up and met my eyes. A genuine smile covered her face, and she walked over to the nearby clothing rack to pick out a new outfit. With her arms loaded, she returned to the dressing room, her smile still intact.

When she came out again, I'm speechless. She's not Stacy anymore. She's... someone else. She's wearing baggy jeans, a loose t-shirt, and a backward baseball hat. But that's not what made her look like someone else. It's the confidence she walked out of the dressing room with. It's the pride in her eyes while she stared at her image in the mirror.

Of course, Stacy didn't buy any of the clothes, and neither did I. We met up with my older sister in the food court after that and never talked about it again. And now I'm wondering... did Stacy struggle with her own identity?

"So," the DDTJ is saying, "we have families with transgender children being investigated, specifically because the children are transgender, to find out if they're providing gender-affirming care." Gender-affirming. I let the phrase roll around in my mind for a minute and wonder how that might have impacted Stacy.

"And there's the threat of prosecution if people *don't* report these families," he continues. I think about Stacy's face when she tried on that outfit and wonder if gender-affirming care would have made that look on her face more permanent.

Unfortunately, I'll never get to find out.

He also paints a bleak picture of trans youth who may have struggled and felt in crisis from their identity struggle, and although they've found a way to manage with medical guidance, these laws come in and say, "Nope. What we say is more important than what your doctor says." I've read that transgender youth can be given puberty blockers to delay the onset of puberty. I've also read they can take estrogen and testosterone—all with entirely reversible effects.

"And we know that when kids don't have this kind of care when they aren't supported this way, the suicide rates go up by at least 50%. We have research and data that *proves* gender-affirming care saves lives, but these bills don't care about that."

The ACLU attorney explains how these bills are a response to efforts towards a more inclusive curriculum that presents a more accurate picture of history. Because of all the protests and demands for Americans to reckon with American history since 2020, there are already laws in effect banning the conversation of race and anything that might make someone feel uncomfortable. Most of the laws about race also mention issues of sex and gender.

It seems to always boil down to the same thing: the people who have been in power want to remain in power, but they can only do so by controlling things like access to information, gender-affirming healthcare, and preventing access to abortion. Each of these items seems like their own separate issue, but they aren't. The current people in power can't remain in power unless they exert their control over the younger generation. If they don't learn to control them now, how will they still benefit when the younger generation obtains control?

Is the ACLU right? Is it really all about power?

Are people really causing suicide rates to rise among transgender youth because their *power* is threatened?

It seems like every piece of land in the world was fought over and stolen from someone at some point. Slavery really existed. I suppose admitting this and paying the price for it would cause *some* loss of power for *someone*. But I imagine it would help more people than it would hurt.

And gender-affirming care—how could that possibly threaten someone's power? How does following the medical guidance of a respected physician cause someone to lose power? How could reducing the rate of suicides be a bad thing? I'm trying not to feel utterly helpless, but my mind keeps returning to Stacy and Jax. How could someone try to pass a law that could so profoundly wound a young person?

I'm not sure how the average person would be able to do anything to fight what's happening, but the ACLU does offer a few suggestions. Unfortunately, the easiest to take action is also the most impossible to implement: disrupting the transgender narrative and eliminating disinformation. This seems like an easy first step, but we just implemented policies at our school that don't allow us to say *anything* about gender identity.

At the elementary level, not discussing any LGBTQ+ relationships means some kids don't get to talk about their families. Everything students do at the elementary school level is centered around their families and communities. What happens to the student with two moms or two dads? Essentially, kids get the message that it's not okay to talk about having two moms or two dads—the message that their family is unacceptable.

How do you tell a child their parents are unacceptable—simply for being together? How do you say to a five-year-old that they can't bring both their dads to the "Dad's and Doughnuts" events the school hosts because it might make other people uncomfortable?

I certainly don't have any of the answers, and it sounds like the ACLU doesn't have many either. Although I'm grateful for their work, I wonder if the ACLU will ever become obsolete. I wonder if society will ever figure out how to treat all humans with kindness and dignity so that we don't need organizations that exist to protect civil liberties.

I make a mental note to investigate some of the other options the ACLU mentioned to get involved, like showing up with food and water for protestors. That one sounds the most realistic until I imagine myself showing up with a cooler full of food to a group of strangers... and then I realize that's the *least* realistic option.

At the end of the virtual town hall, I feel more lost than hopeful. I'm glad to know there are tons of professionals working around the clock to preserve fundamental human rights for LGBTQ+ community members. Still, my heart hurts knowing that these laws are even being introduced. It hurts my heart to think someone could investigate Jax's mom for child abuse or that Jax's doctor could go to prison for providing health care to them. I wish I could protect them all.

Sunday mornings are for coffee and grading, apparently. Well, I am not exactly grading. I haven't given any actual assignments yet to have anything to grade, but these nameplate conversations are taking a good amount of time. I curl up in the big beige armchair next to my bed with my stack of nameplates and trusty Flair pen. The first nameplate is Jax's, and I open it first.

Thanks for making it safe to be me.

I feel a slight ache in my chest reading Jax's comment to me. I really want to say something special and meaningful because I know they're having a rough time with the dress code stuff. Being nonbinary and figuring out who you are is challenging enough without being a freshman in high school getting dress coded for potentially distracting males. I feel a bit of adrenaline starting to pump in my veins as I think about it all.

I write my carefully thought-out response: *You deserve to feel safe being you— everywhere.* Students being themselves shouldn't be a safety hazard. It also shouldn't put a target on a student's back for things like dress code. I can't help but wonder how many of the other, less conspicuous-looking students get dress coded and how often. I think about all the students with cannabis logos and leaves on their clothing and wonder if they get dress coded as often.

I've always known there were tons of glaring inconsistencies and double standards in education, given that I went through the public education system myself. Still, I don't particularly appreciate seeing it in action. Especially since I'm a first-year teacher and I have to keep my mouth shut if I want to stay employed.

I try to put the thoughts of Jax in the back of my brain and continue reading and responding to some of the student's questions and comments.

I play GTA5, and I like to help randoms make quick money $$$.

I have so many questions I don't know where to begin. I respond with, "*What is GTA5? And how do you make money?*"

Another student writes, "*My favorite YouTuber is Mr. THC. What is your favorite YouTuber?*

I can't stop my eyes from rolling and promptly pick up my phone to search for Mr. THC. As I'm traversing through his Instagram and YouTube, I see an absurd amount of marijuana. Then, I realized this was exactly what I expected from a YouTuber called "Mr. THC."

I guess I was just hoping it would be something else…

Maybe he was really Mr. Totally Hot Cop, and this student was just learning how to be an impressive police officer. Or perhaps Mr. THC stood for Mr. Troubling Homework Collective, where kids go to discuss troubling homework assignments that they need help with...

I try to think of something appropriate to say and wonder if I'm supposed to report this. With all the kids walking around campus with cannabis leaves, I doubt this would be shocking to anyone. I reply, *"Thanks for sharing! In the future, let's keep anything related to drugs and alcohol separate from class assignments. Also, what's YouTube?"* I add the last part as a joke. I don't watch YouTube, so I can't answer his question anyway. I also don't want to reprimand a student and prevent them from connecting with me later on.

The following paper is less interesting: *"Hi, can you tell me what my email is?"* I grab a yellow post-it from the nightstand between my armchair and my bed and make a note to follow up on the student's email address.

I continue reading and replying:

You know drinking coffee means eating cockroaches, right?

Okay, this one just about knocks me out of my seat. I suppose there are probably cockroaches in lots of processed foods... and I also believe I need a new line of thinking before I ruin the best part of my day every day. In response to the student, I write:

-Why would you tell me this???

The next one I come across makes up for the gross cockroach discussion.

Fun fact: I actually really like this class and feel comfortable.

-That IS a fun fact! I'm so happy to hear that!

With my spirits lifted, I'm able to get through the rest of my stack in about a half-hour. I learned about some of my students' favorite candies, and animes to watch. I learned many students enjoyed my class this week and got a lot of comments about being welcoming. As I put the cap back on my pen, I feel more satisfaction and fulfillment than I've felt in a long time. Maybe more than I've ever felt before. Knowing that I made students feel welcome, knowing that Jax feels safe in my room, and having these mini one-on-one conversations with each student… they all feel like significant wins.

The following week is more tedious procedures and routines. A full day is spent introducing the "Shipman High Way" of doing things to students. This included fire drills, lockdowns, tardy policies, and practice logging into school email.

On Wednesday morning, I see one of my first-period students, Jasper, wandering the halls. It's 7:20, and the campus isn't open to students until 7:30. I make sure to make eye contact with Jasper and say hello. He's another student on my roster I haven't seen much during the last week and a half. It's great to see him on campus so early. Unfortunately, I didn't realize that would be the last time I would see him that week. He never showed up to my class.

The last two days of the week are spent administering diagnostic tests for the various websites we'll use throughout the school year. All in all, very unexciting.

However, I did get to use all that time during the diagnostics to plan my lessons for the next month. Well, I really just copied and pasted Penny's lesson plans, but I think it still counts. I searched the internet for interesting supplemental materials I might want for the upcoming weeks, but I couldn't find anything. I'm not even sure what I'm supposed to be teaching for most of the year. I was given a set of the Common Core English standards broken up into four quarters, but that was it. I was told I had complete autonomy to teach anything I wanted (within reason, of course). The problem is that I don't know *what* to teach as a first-year teacher. Penny was kind enough to offer me her lesson plans to copy until I got my footing.

So, for the next three weeks, my students will be reading a series of speeches that will hopefully help them transition into their roles as scholars. We will work on the Jane Schaffer writing method with each article, which I've never heard of. So, I spent most of my weekend Googling Jane Schaffer and what made her method special. I didn't find any answers for the special part, but I did walk away with the solid understanding that it seems like any other formula for paragraph writing.

We start with David Foster Wallace's *"This Is Water"* commencement address. It's a long speech that begins with a parable of an old fish swimming by some younger fish and asking, *"How's the water today?"* And the younger fish replied, *"What is water?"* Throughout the speech, Wallace offers a different perspective of life and what it means to *think*. I made sure to make copies for each student to annotate, and I'm excited to see what the students think. I realize I won't be able to afford to do this often, but it seemed like the first assignment of the year requiring annotation should be done and taught on paper.

When I first hand the speech out to each of my regular English 9 classes, the reactions are much the same: a skeptical look at the packet followed by an incredulous look at me, followed by another skeptical look at the thick packet.

It didn't take much for me to realize they weren't used to sustained silent—or otherwise—reading at all. I had thought I could give the students the packet and a highlighter and let them go. It's not looking like that's going to work, though.

After my first class period of the day stared at the first page of the packet for a full 30 minutes without actually reading a single word, I realized I'd have to read it to them. Before reading it aloud, I asked if any students thought it would be helpful. Nearly every hand in the room shot up in response, yet none of them had asked for help or indicated they were struggling. They just… sat there.

In the second class period that I teach the same lesson, I find an audio recording of the speech and play it for the students—all 22 minutes of it. Halfway through, I realize I have lost more than half the class, but I don't know what to do, so I just let the audio play through. By the time it's finished, three students are sleeping.

The third and final time I taught it, I decided to just dig into it the way I would if I were alone. I ask students comprehension questions about each paragraph, have them underline the main ideas, and put question marks next to words they don't know. By the end of the first page, students have marked nearly a dozen words with question marks. I finally started to realize why my students had been falling asleep. This might as well be written in a different language for what the students are getting out of it.

We make it through the first two pages, but I'm not sure the students even understand what we discussed. I give them the last 10 minutes of class as free time so that I can sulk at my desk about this awful lesson.

While sitting at my desk and reflecting, I watch the commotion among the students. One student takes his shoes off and trades them with different students around the room. Two girls are doing TikTok dances by my bookshelf, and the rest seem to be occupied with their phones. A quieter student, Rudy, walks up to my desk, drops a folded piece of paper, then turns and walks away without saying anything.

I opened the folded paper and read the pencil scratchings inside.

Dear Ms. White,

I'm sorry to bother you, but I wanted to ask if you could please move my seat. I really don't like sitting next to Marie and her friends. They're always putting people down and making fun of them. Also, please don't say anything about this note. I really don't want to be on her bad side.

-Rudy

I look up at Rudy after reading the note, but he's sitting silently at his desk with his head down. I realize that he sits directly in front of Marie, who happens to be here today. I had no idea that Rudy was uncomfortable or that Marie even talked during class. Usually, she just stares at her phone. But I add *seating charts* to my to-do list.

After hearing how students talk to each other, I decided we needed some sort of classroom pact. During the first week of school, I reviewed my three classroom rules: be respectful, responsible, and ready to learn. Unfortunately, introducing these as classroom rules didn't seem to have done much good. Students are still constantly slapping each other on the back of the neck (apparently, this is a requirement among teenage males), calling things they don't like 'gay,' and just having generally bad attitudes.

Of course, this doesn't describe all the students, but it's enough to get me to spend some time researching how to create a more welcoming classroom. I come across all kinds of great stuff on Pinterest and Edutopia and eventually decide to make a classroom pact with my students. I was worried about how much time this would take away from academics, so I emailed Penny for permission before putting the lesson together. I was advised that, in the future, these types of lessons should be done during the first week of school. It felt like a bit of a reprimand.

"Alright, lovely humans! Today we're going to figure out how we want to be treated in class, and *you guys* are going to create our classroom contract," I say enthusiastically in front of my 7th period honor's class. I decided to use them as my guinea pigs for this lesson because they tend to be better behaved than my regular students.

They don't moan and groan about the activity as I had expected, and I decide to take this as a sign that I'm heading in the right direction with classroom management. I tell everyone to take out a piece of paper and write their answers to the following questions:

1. How do I want to be treated by my peers?

2. How do I think my peers want to be treated by me?
3. How do I want to be treated by my teacher?
4. How do I think my teacher wants to be treated by me?

I give the students about 10 minutes before introducing each succeeding question and ask them to share with their shoulder partner and then with the class as a whole. All anyone can come up with is the word 'respect.' Everybody wants to be treated with respect. From here, I realize I've hit a dead end. I just spent almost an entire class period on an activity that produced a *single-word* answer from the majority of the students.

I ask the students to work with a partner to develop the two most important class rules they think should be implemented. But really, I'm just trying to buy time to figure out what to do now that our only rules will be vague and less than meaningful.

While the students work together to develop some of the rules they deem most important, I brainstorm ways to make this activity more concrete, and it hits me—we need examples and non-examples.

In true new teacher fashion, I stopped the students from working on the rules I had just assigned and instead wrote the word *RESPECT* in the middle of the whiteboard.

"If you were to walk into a classroom, how would you know everyone in the room really respected each other? What does respect in the classroom look like?" I ask hopefully.

Nobody says anything, and I provide an awkward amount of wait time before asking again, "What would you see if you walked into a classroom where everyone respected each other?"

Finally, a quiet-looking boy hesitantly raises his hand—not even confident enough to raise it above his shoulder. I give him the warmest and most encouraging smile I can muster in hopes that the other students will want to participate as well as a result. "Yes! Cal!"

"People paying attention?" he asks hesitantly.

"Are you asking me or telling me?" I ask, trying to encourage him to be confident in his answer.

"Um…" He thinks about it for a second. "I'm telling you."

"Awesome! Yes! If you walked into a classroom where everyone respected everyone, you would see people paying attention to whoever had the floor. Great answer, Cal." I jot down his answer on the board before asking for more.

Other students start volunteering answers without raising their hands, and I'm so happy they're participating; I don't think I could possibly care less about how much hand raising I see.

"No cell phones," another student suggests. The class "oohs" in unison, and I'm impressed that freshman students understand that being on their phones during class disrupts their work and disrespects whoever is working for their attention. I add the suggestion to the board.

We continue jotting down ideas until the class is silent again. Then, I ask them what respect sounds like. Students volunteer the typical answers of using manners, saying "please" and "thank you," and a distinct lack of swear words.

I repeat the process with the students for what respect feels like, then ask the kids to spend the remainder of class working on their two most essential class rules. Just as we're finishing up, I see Marie raise her hand.

Marie, my disappearing Houdini from last week, has her hand up. I call on her enthusiastically, eager to see her participate voluntarily.

"That's not respect," she says with a blank face.

"What do you mean?" I ask.

"All that stuff you wrote up there—that's not respect. That's not what respect is."

In college, they didn't prepare me to respond to students who challenged my lesson, so naturally, my adrenaline started pumping. Somehow, I'm in fight or flight mode again, and I try to stay present for the conversation.

"Okay, what do *you* think is a good definition of respect?"

I ask her.

She's silent and looks irritated.

After a prolonged silence with the whole class staring at her, she says, "Never mind. Nothing."

"Are you sure?" I ask. I'm not too fond of her attitude or how she's going about whatever she's trying to do, but I want her to have the same opportunity to voice her opinions as the other students. "If you have a different definition for respect, I'd love to hear it."

"No, it's fine," she says with her arms crossed over her chest.

"Okay…" I trail off but then encourage the class to get back on task.

While they work with their shoulder partners, I circulate the room. Marie sits alone and refuses to work with anyone. She hasn't taken out a piece of paper or participated in any of the activities for the day.

She hasn't had much to say in class, but she's had plenty to say through text messages to whoever she has on her phone. I casually make my way through each group of students until I make it to Marie, where she sits at a group of desks but is alone and on her phone.

"Marie, can you come sit with this group over here? That way, you have someone to talk to."

"No, I'm fine," she says without so much as a glance away from her phone.

"I'm glad you're fine, but you are getting points for this assignment. You haven't even taken out paper today, so I'm a little concerned."

"I'm gonna do it when I get home."

Sure, yeah. She's going to go home and discuss with her friends and family the definition of respect and what that looks like in a classroom. A classroom where she declared the student-generated definition of respect inaccurate at best. She still doesn't look away from her phone.

"You know, for someone with an opinion about respect,

you sure aren't showing much respect right now." I'm not sure what I'm hoping by making this observation out loud, but I feel it can't be worse than *not* trying to talk to her.

Just then, the bell rings. Before I can even begin to wrap up the lesson, students have packed up and already walked out the door. As soon as it rings, Marie stands up and walks out—never having taken her backpack off her shoulders and phone in hand. She doesn't look at me or say goodbye as she leaves.

"See you Thursday!" I shout after her, knowing it won't make a difference.

Once all the students have left my room, I pull up my student info spreadsheet and document the conversation with Marie. I then decide to be brave and call Marie's parents. I figure a student disagreeing with an entire class on a broad definition of respect might indicate troubles on the horizon.

I pull up the Google Voice app on my phone and dial the number listed in Marie's student profile. A woman's voice answers.

"Hello?"

"Hi, can I please speak to the parent or guardian of Marie Banks?" I try to sound pleasant, but I'm feeling a little nervous.

"This is she."

"Hi, I'm Marie's English teacher, Ms. White. I was just calling because I've been having difficulty getting Marie to participate in class. Last week, she left for the restroom and never returned. And today she only participated to announce that she disagreed with the class' definition of respect. I'm wondering if there's something I can do to help her feel more comfortable in the class." I try to sound concerned but confident and hope my voice doesn't betray me.

"That's just Marie. That's just the way she is. She's an only child, and she's like that with everyone. It's nothing personal against you."

I'm shocked that the response to her daughter ditching and refusing to participate in class is, *"That's just Marie."* How do a parent and child get to a point where the child can't manage in class, and the parent's only response is, *"that's just her"*?

"Well, could you tell me about her hobbies or the kind of music she likes? Maybe I can try to connect with her over something like that..." My voice trails off while my brain continues its frenzy of figuring out how to be an adult human on an actual phone call.

"All she does is watch TikTok and dance. That's all she cares about. TikTok and dance."

"Oh… Okay…" I'm feeling stupider by the minute. At what point do I end the call? Is this really the only method of communication parents had with teachers before text messages? This awkward, vocal exchange with no time to think or process before each response? I feel bad for people who grew up in the 90's.

"Well," I finally conclude, "thank you for your help. Hopefully, Marie and I can get off to a new start next week and go from there."

"Alright. Good luck."

"Thanks." I hung up the phone and documented it in my spreadsheet. I guess the next time I see Marie, I'll be asking her who she follows on TikTok. And then, I will Google them because I don't know how to use TikTok. So much for the benefit of being a young teacher…

12

Once we've made it through the tediousness that was the first unit Penny picked out, I feel confident enough to stray from her lesson plans and try something I find on Teachers Pay Teachers. The assignment aligns with Common Core standards and allows students to be super creative. The students get to curate the soundtracks to their own lives based on their experiences. Plus, students kept asking to continue the nameplate back-and-forth notes. I really enjoyed getting to know the students over the last several weeks, and this will continue that trend.

I start the lesson by sharing the first three songs of my soundtrack. The first song is AJR's "Birthday Party" because who isn't optimistic when they're little? The second song on my soundtrack is "Shake a Tail Feather" because it was one of my favorite songs as a kid. When my dad played it, I always danced around the house. I also grew up with birds, so this song made me feel like my birds were dancing with me. The third song on my soundtrack is "Thunder" by Imagine Dragons because I always knew that I would do something great, despite what others might have told me.

I share this as an example of how the students will use the Jane Schaffer paragraph structure to explain how each song relates to their lives. They quote a line from the song and explain how it relates to a moment in their lives. They will do one paragraph a week for the rest of the quarter.

I pass out the planning sheets for the activity along with a handout for students to design the cover of their soundtrack. While I pass out the papers, I get to see the students eagerly discussing their favorite songs and asking each other for song suggestions. I'm absolutely elated to see so many students interacting with each other; I don't even notice that half the class seems to miss the point about the songs being meaningful and related to a specific event or moment in their lives.

I do notice one of my students, Colleen, watching YouTube and TikTok videos. I stand over her shoulder for a moment to see if she's just momentarily distracted, but she seems fully enthralled by the content on her phone.

"Hey, Colleen, I need you to be on task right now."

She doesn't even bother to look up from her phone but says, "I'll do it for homework."

"You're going to waste an entire class period doing nothing so you can do what you should have done at home during your free time?" I ask, trying to sound as shocked as I feel.

"Yes," she says, eyes still glued to her phone.

I have no idea how to respond to her. The logic behind this decision is entirely beyond me, so I just walk away. I'm really not sure what else I can do. I suppose as long as she does the assignment at some point, I should just be happy…

By the end of the day, I have no real sense of whether or not the students will struggle with the activity, but I'm excited nonetheless. I love getting to learn about the students and the songs they love. I dream of having clips from a bunch of their favorite songs that I can push a button and just play on demand. My university once had a guest speaker that had tons of songs cued up and ready to go. Throughout his presentation, he would constantly play song clips over the speakers. It really engaged the room.

In reality, I have a sad Spotify playlist with a couple of clean and cheerful songs I play during class. I hope this activity will give me some new stuff to add to my playlist to engage the students.

Oliver raises his hand to ask if he can use the restroom. I write him the requisite pass, then don't see him again for the rest of the day.

At the end of the week, I excitedly remove each stack of paragraphs from the corresponding period's tray. By the third week of school, I had realized I was wasting tons of class time just passing out and collecting papers. So, when I got my first paycheck, I made a point to pick up the things I needed the most. I decided that having trays for students to turn their work into would be an inexpensive way to improve my quality of life considerably. I was mostly correct; it was more expensive than I had anticipated.

I bring the stack back to my desk and turn on the mini powder blue Keurig on the bookshelf next to it. I also decided with my first paycheck that having coffee during class time would make me a better teacher, so I *had* to buy a Keurig. I place my favorite *"I Like Big Books & I Cannot Lie"* mug under the coffee drip and hit start.

While the coffee brews, I try to make myself comfortable in my desk's sad, broken blue chair. The quarter-inch of fabric covering the seat portion doesn't seem to make it any more comfortable than it would be without the material, and I find myself wondering about its purpose. This is the stupid stuff my mind expends energy on. I spent three minutes wondering about the fabric on a cheap plastic chair that I *could have* spent grading an assignment.

I try to physically shake the last thought out of my head,

grab my fresh-brewed cup of coffee, and mentally prepare to focus.

The first paper I pick up happens to belong to Oliver. I find it interesting that he ditches class but still manages to get his assignments turned in. Oliver has chosen "Stressed Out" by Twenty One Pilots. He writes:

I chose this song because it represents my whole life. The song mentions missing the old days when our mothers would sing us to sleep. My mom used to sing me to sleep at night, but she died of cancer when I was 8. I'm always wishing I could turn back time.

I'm seriously impressed with Oliver's response. I'm impressed that a kid who spends so little time in class could make a connection and convey it in writing. I'm also really, really sad for him. I can't imagine losing a parent that young—especially my mom. I wonder how much this impacts Oliver's classroom behavior.

The following paper I pick up is from another student of mine in first period, Beatrice. Beatrice is incredibly quiet and rarely talks or participates. She usually wears dark eyeliner, dark lipstick, and remarkably thick fake lashes. She also has fake nails that are easily two inches long. She writes:

The first song on my soundtrack would be 'Rumors' by Lizzo because it always makes me happy when I hear it. Lizzo always knows what's up.

Although I'd love to bond with her over our shared love of Lizzo, I'm concerned that her "paragraph" is only two sentences. Additionally, she didn't explain how the song relates to a moment in her life. Shipman High School has a strict policy that all work turned in earns a minimum of 60%, and assignments not turned in earn a minimum of 50%. Well, I don't know if "earn" is the right word to use here...

I give Beatrice the mandatory 60% and move on to the next one. I get to Cody's paper and see that he's chosen *Eye of the Tiger* as the first song on his soundtrack.

I chose Eye of the Tiger by Survivor because it's

motivational. The song makes me feel like I can do anything, so I listen to it at least once a day. I always feel really good after.

As I read through Cody's paper, I see the need for Jane Schaffer instruction. All of the paragraphs are missing direct quotes; some are missing a significant connection to a life event, and some paragraphs aren't even... *paragraphs.* I pull up my to-do list on my cell phone and add Jane Schaffer lesson plans to my list.

I get through most of my first period's assignments before finally coming across Jax's. I have been incredibly curious to see what songs they might pick. By the eclectic way Jax dresses and acts, I can't even begin to predict the type of the music they enjoy. I eagerly read:

The first song on the soundtrack of my life would be "Same Love" by Macklemore. In the song, Macklemore says he thought he was gay because of his similarities to his gay uncle. This line reminds me of being a kid and watching my female cousins play dress-up. They loved dressing up in my mom's old stuff, and they would try to get me to dress up with them. I always hated it because they thought I was a girl. I didn't feel like a girl. I was just me.

The song also says comments on how America used to be called brave, but it's scared of what it doesn't understand. This reminds me of how weird people are about gender. People who aren't part of the LGBTQ+ community only have hateful things to say, but they don't know anything about the community. Why don't they try to get to know people?

Finally, the song says that we've forgotten that God loves all His children. I think this is where we are now. In elementary school I had a lot of friends that were religious. Now, none of my Christian friends will hang out with me or even talk to me.

Oh, Jax. My heart is heavy for them. I guess I thought my LGBTQ+ students would be more oblivious to the world. I'm not sure which part of their assignment bums me out the most. Thinking about Jax as a kid who wasn't allowed to fit in...or becoming a teenager who still isn't allowed to fit in. It just isn't fair.

I finish the first period's assignments by 4:00 on a Friday and decide the rest will come home with me.

Before I head home, I decide to make a few parent contacts. I pull up my Student Info spreadsheet and highlight the students whose parents I need to contact still. I've made it a point to start jotting down notes about the positive things I see students do, as well as something positive to mention to the families of my quieter students. I never want a student to feel invisible or in any way overlooked. What if Stacy had had that?

I think about Oliver leaving class today and debate over contacting his home. On the one hand, he technically ditched class by not returning. On the other hand, it was towards the end of the period, and students were far more productive once he left. Do I write him up? Tell his parents? Or just overlook it and try to track student bathroom use more closely?

I decided that since Oliver had turned in his assignment, I'll let it slide this time. Instead, I focus on all the kids calling each other gay and using it as an insult. It seems like the more comfortable students get in class, the more comfortable they are saying unkind or cruel things. I decided to type a generic message for the parents of these students and copy and paste it to each one through the Remind application on my phone.

The message read: *Hi, this is your student's English teacher, Ms. White, from Shipman High. I wanted to let you know that I've had to talk to _________ about using the word 'gay' as an insult in class. Please follow up with them and let me know if you have any questions.*

After I type out the message, I add each student's individual name before pasting the message into each parent's texting box on the Remind app. Before I hit send, I take a second to reread the message and see if it sounds professional. I'm worried about parents getting upset, but I also wonder if I can cite the new school policies as reasons that it's unacceptable if I get any push back. I guess I will have to wait and see.

13

Walking into Diogo Kaufman's room for the next PLC meeting is far more exciting than it should be. His classroom is halfway across campus, but it's worth the walk. His room is a portable bungalow, so it's far from the rest of us. When I finally get to his portable, I knock loudly on the door. Within moments he opens it with his perfectly wind-blown hair, and his green eyes are beaming.

"Samantha, welcome. Come on in," he says casually. I pull the door the rest of the way open and follow him inside. His portable is dimly lit with three different floor lamps around the room. The overhead lights remain off. The desks are all in pods of 4 facing the whiteboard at the front of the room. I smell a hint of patchouli and vanilla, which adds a comforting feel to the room. He has several beanbags and floor pillows on the left side of the room. A few small Ikea tables are placed intermittently, and positive affirmations are posted around the room.

I sit in one of the pods near the front of the room and steal nervous glances at Diogo's gorgeous face and perfect teeth whenever the opportunity presents itself. I seem always to be the first person to our PLC meetings, and I make a note to fix that in the future. I pull out my phone and start scanning Facebook while waiting for my colleagues to join me. As my eyes see the latest updates in war, teaching, and fashion, I realize a faint humming or buzzing sound is in the background. I can't quite figure out what it is or where it's coming from.

"Do you hear that?" I ask, sounding as confused as I felt.

"The binaural beats?"

"Is that what's playing in the background?"

"It is! I have it on all day for my students," he says. I can't imagine having to listen to this odd humming-buzzing sound and give a quick nod in response.

"It's been scientifically proven to change brainwaves in listeners to help them exist in a more calm, meditative state. It can reduce anxiety in students," he adds.

This piques my interest, even if it sounds a little too "New Age-y" for my taste. I inspect his room a little more carefully, half expecting to find lava lamps about the room.

"How long have you been teaching?" I ask him as casually as I can. I try not to look at him so I can remember how to breathe and act like a professional.

"This is actually my second year," he says. "How about you?"

"This is my *first* year," I say. "Any words of wisdom for a newbie?"

He chuckles at this, and his gorgeous, wide smile reaches each ear. His eyes practically light up against his perfect umber skin, and I'm suddenly quoting Shakespeare in my head.

Sometimes, I still can't believe someone gave me a teaching license.

Emma and Giselle walk in together, with Penny trailing behind. None of them are speaking or look particularly comfortable being so close to one another. I wonder if it's because Penny is the department chair or if there's something deeper going on.

Emma and Giselle take a seat at the same pod as me. I'm secretly thrilled that someone has chosen to sit near me in an entirely empty classroom. Being the new teacher is much like being the new student at a school. You have no idea where the bathrooms are, can't remember anyone's names, and you're pretty sure you forget *something* at all times. Being the newbie is rough.

Diogo comes to the pod to join us, which is a little awkward. Four full-grown adults are sitting at a small pod of student desks in a vast empty classroom… with Penny standing a few feet in front of us.

"Alright, everyone, we're going to watch the first two minutes of each of the videos listed on the Supplemental Text Google form and give a *very official* thumbs up or down for each item. Give me a thumbs up if you understand," Penny adds jokingly, inciting a pity chuckle from Diogo.

She walks back to Diogo's desk, signs in to her Google account, and projects the Google spreadsheet for all of us to see. I first notice that there are at least three dozen entries by Emma alone. The form has columns for the link to the supplemental text, its purpose, and the standards it meets. Several of the videos have lengthy explanations and multiple standards tied to them.

I turn around to look at Penny out of curiosity. This is supposed to be a 25-minute meeting, but there's no way we'd get through all of these in 25 minutes. To my surprise, Penny has a smile plastered on her face. I can't tell if she's actually happy, though, because she doesn't seem to be blinking. Instead, she looks like one of those creepy children's dolls with eyelids that only close when lying down.

I turn back to the board in time to see her scrolling through the rest of the list. There are 87 entries total. I hear her sigh loudly from the back of the room, followed by her cheerful voice saying, "Okay, let's get started!"

The first link she clicks is an entry from Diogo. She lets the video play for a full two minutes before stopping. The video seems to be live footage of an ocean with waves lapping the shore every few 60 seconds or so with a background of binaural beats.

Next to the video, Diego explained that the video's purpose is for meditation. He links some speaking standards and explains that the meditation helps students "come to discussions prepared," and I'm impressed with his reasoning. I'm not sure Penny agrees, but she did say we got to vote as a PLC. Penny asks everyone to give a thumbs up or down for the resource, and all four of us have thumbs in the air.

"Okay, on to the next one," Penny says with slightly less pep. The second video is another meditation video from Diogo. This time he's linked some writing standards he plans to use while having students free-write with the video on in the background. Penny has a more challenging time letting this one play for a full two minutes, but something about the binaural beats and Cherry Blossom trees blowing softly in the wind must have pulled her in. She asks for another vote, and the four of us remain unanimous.

After five of Diogo's meditation videos for the upcoming week, it's 3:25, and we're all incredibly sleepy from the extended amounts of meditation.

"Diogo, your kids don't fall asleep?" Emma asks him with an appropriate amount of surprise in her voice, given our current state.

"Well, yeah, of course they do…" he says, letting his voice trail off.

And this is his second year teaching.

"If the kids fall asleep, why do you keep doing it?" she presses.

"I figure they must need someplace to rest. Kids don't always get to rest at home. At least they can rest here."

I wonder if he also does yoga with his students.

"Alright guys, that means afternoon naps will be hosted here in Diogo's room. So, if you can make it to the portables during that 4-minute passing period, you've got your resting place," Giselle declares.

"Oh, absolutely! You guys are welcome any time. Come on down any time you need a break or want to say hi," Diogo responds.

I can't tell if everyone is entirely genuine in the conversation, but that's probably because I haven't gotten to know anyone well enough yet. I find it really, *really* hard not to make jokes about Diogo's room and the meditation videos.

I love that he cares about his students so much and that he's had the time to find and request approval for so many meditation videos. I think it's bizarre that he does so much meditation with his students when I can't seem to manage to get through my entire agenda most days, but I also realize I'm a first-year teacher. I don't know everything—even if I sometimes feel like I do.

One of my favorite mentors from college used to tell me that the best teachers know they're never *the best*. The best teachers are constantly learning, reflecting, and improving. I wrote that on the inside of my binder during my teaching observations to remind myself. It's become my mantra for teaching.

"Alright, everyone," Penny stands at Diogo's desk in the back and makes her way through the pods of desks to the front. "We're obviously not going to be able to get through all 87 of these, and I'm not sure what to do."

"We could all use Kaufman's mediation videos!" Emma offers with fake enthusiasm. Everyone chuckles, and the tension seems to ease a bit.

"You guys, there are 87 links. How are there 87?" Penny seems slightly frustrated—which is the angriest I've ever seen her.

"You said *every single* supplemental text, video clip, article, etc. You wanted *every single* one, and you got *every single* one.

If anything, I think it's impressive as hell that our PLC is so on-the-ball with this new mandate. We're killing it, guys." Emma seems to make a lot of jokes that seem like they could be either serious or sarcastic. Her smile, however, is constant and looks entirely genuine. Like Penny, she seems to be a person impossible to hate.

Penny's responding smile looked slightly less genuine, but then she sighed, let her shoulders slump, and said, "I guess you're right. This is a good thing. The fact that we can get 87 supplemental texts listed in just two weeks proves that there are hundreds of supplemental texts our kids are getting access to daily that parents know nothing about. And it shows that getting on board with the mandate is possible. If our PLC can get our butts in gear and get this many items in two weeks, the other departments can, too."

Penny's genuine smile has returned, and she stands tall with her shoulders straight. She seems to have convinced herself that this was all a good thing. She says a quick goodbye to everyone and leaves the portable. Emma and Giselle are laughing hard once the door has shut behind her.

I desperately want to be part of the joke, but I'm unsure how to do it politely. While they continue their conversation, I pretend to gather my phone, keys, and pens into my teacher's bag.

"Damn, Em, you've been busy," Giselle says while trying to contain a laugh.

"Well, if they want every supplemental text, they will get *every* supplemental text."

"You realize we're going to have to watch every single one of those videos and vote on them," Giselle asks with her eyebrows raised, giving Emma a sort of *"I hope you thought this through"* look.

"Good, maybe it will keep us so busy, we won't have time to report on LGBTQ+ students," Emma responds with sass. "At least that's the plan. I included anything I could ever possibly want to use and ensured every single one was tied to a standard. I also… may have… included some that I would obviously never use, so that should make the review sessions a little more interesting," Emma adds.

I stifle a giggle and try to find another reason to remain in the classroom a little longer so I can continue to listen in on their conversation.

"Eventually, Penny will realize that this is a ridiculous and unnecessary undertaking. Eventually, she will see how impossible it is to police anything and everything happening in any classroom. I know she has kids, and I know she's worried about their future. But I'm worried about our current students. They deserve access to the same information the rest of the world has access to."

"Dang, Em. Tell me how you *really* feel about it," Giselle says.

Emma rolls her eyes and says, "I have to get to basketball practice. Are you stopping by the game tonight?"

"Wouldn't miss it!" Giselle adds as the two start to walk out of the portable.

Dismayed, I realize I'm alone again with Diogo and decide to stop my ruse of pretending to be packing up. I grab my bag by the straps to heave it onto my shoulder when I hear a loud snapping sound. The strap breaks and my bag falls, tumbling its contents onto the ground.

Oh good, I think to myself, *I have an audience for this embarrassment.*

I look over to see if Diogo has noticed the scene I'm making, and he's sitting at his desk, staring at me.

"Dude," he says slowly, "Bummer."

Clearly, it was his love of poetry that prompted him to become a teacher. Or maybe it was his ability to be concise and observant rather than actively helpful.

I'm unbelievably embarrassed and frantically shovel the contents of my bag back inside. Once it's done, I gather the bag awkwardly in my arms and say, "Have a good night, Mr. Kaufman," and walk out of the portable.

One of these days, I'm going to learn to talk to human adults and not be a bumbling idiot. Until then, I guess I'll just keep talking to my students.

When I make it back to my classroom, I think my arms might fall off. I remember the rolling cart suggested to me and made another mental note to put it on my shopping list. And since it's a mental note, I'm sure to forget it until the next time I desperately wish I had one. It's the subtle predictability in my life that keeps me from going crazy.

I drop my overstuffed bag on the desk nearest the door and walk to my computer. I have to ensure I haven't gotten any emails regarding my lessons for the following few weeks. I'm woefully behind on much of the planning, so I just keep using what Penny has. And since we have 87 supplemental text entries to review, I can't imagine any of my entries being approved in time to use them. The thought of this is a little disheartening. I'm just starting the school year, and I'm already behind.

I sit at my desk and turn on the archaic machine Mr. Wolf called a "computer." While waiting for it to load, I read through a few more nameplates from this week.

"Miss, are you coming to the football scrimmage this Friday?" A student named Jerome has asked me.

I've seen the emails and posters about the Back to School Tailgate for the football team's first scrimmage this year. There will be food trucks for the students and a barbecue for the faculty and staff. They even have the end zone set up for the barbecue. I haven't met anyone I'd be comfortable sitting with yet, and the only family I'd have to bring are my parents, which would be embarrassing. So, I write:

"Unfortunately, no, but are you on the team?" In my Happy Planner, I've created a hand-drawn spreadsheet for notes about students, so I add a note to check in on Jerome's status as an athlete.

I log into my district email once the computer has finally warmed up and the screen is clear. Every time I log into my work email, my stomach is in absolute knots. I'm waiting for a parent or community concern about one of my lesson plans or an email from the admin commenting on something I've done wrong. The new district mandates really have me on edge.

I scroll through my emails and see one from Penny sent right after the PLC meeting.

Hey Team!

Great first round of supplemental text review! I am looking for ideas on making the process quicker and smoother for everyone involved. Please email me your thoughts. In the meantime, remember only to use <u>approved</u> supplemental texts. Please delete any entries we no longer need to preview if we didn't get to your entries this round. Also, let's ensure the standard attached to the supplemental text is obvious within the first two minutes.

*If it isn't, ask yourself if it's **really** necessary.*

Well, I guess that means I'll be using meditative videos to reinforce Jane Schaffer paragraphs. At least I know my students will be relaxed while they're working! I can't complain too much since I didn't have any videos or texts to suggest. That was part of the reason I chose to do the soundtrack activity with my students—it didn't require them to read any supplemental texts that had to be approved.

Even news articles must be approved before we can use them, which makes me wonder. How can they really enforce this? Who would know if a bunch of my students *happened* to read the same online news article? And then I would be able to teach a lesson about it because they would have all read it...

And then I wonder about the penalty for not getting things pre-approved. What would happen if I taught a short story that hadn't yet been approved? What would happen if the students studied a poem that wasn't ever mentioned... would they run to Penny and tell her I taught a poem that's *not* on a list that they don't know exists? Unlikely.

The worst consequence I can think of is being non-reelected next year. Because I don't have tenure, the admin can let me go at any time without having to give me any reason. Hence, the reason everyone tells new teachers to keep their heads down. The price teachers pay for not "falling in line" is unemployment.

I guess we'll be sticking to meditation videos this week.

14

By the middle of October, it seems everyone has settled into the school year. I've figured out that there's less chaos if I have something on the board for students to work on when they enter the room, and the students have figured out that class moves quicker if they participate. They seem more comfortable talking and participating, making teaching much more enjoyable.

I've also learned an unbelievable amount about my students. The weekly paragraphs selecting songs related to their lives revealed more than most students probably intended.

The only problem is that it seems like kids are making gay jokes every day. I'm doing everything I can to mitigate it when it happens, but that doesn't seem to be helping. I texted multiple parents a few weeks ago, and nothing has changed. The same students are still making gay jokes—one even called his friend a "faggot" as a joke. I was beyond shocked. And furious.

I knew I had to do something, so I searched the Learning for Justice database and found a lesson I could implement to improve my classroom environment.

The lesson from Learning For Justice's website that I decided to do is called "What's So Bad About 'That's So Gay'?" I know we aren't allowed to discuss gender or sexual orientation in class, but I figure this lesson has great objectives and important essential questions; surely, a conversation about a harmful saying isn't the same as discussing gender and identity.

The lesson starts with students doing a quick write about a time they've been called a name and how that made them feel. Afterward, I ask for volunteers to share out, and I immediately regret it.

"Whenever my mom calls me a bitch, I just laugh it off," says a student. I'm not prepared to be informed that my student's parent calls her a bitch, so I'm momentarily taken aback and without words.

"Okay..." I say, desperately looking for an appropriate response. "That's... one way to handle that."

Another hand goes up, and this time it belongs to a student named Steve. "People always call me a beaner, and I don't care."

Okay, this isn't going the way I had expected it to. I was hoping they would share stories of being labeled painfully incorrectly or that they had some experience with name-calling. It seems they have experience, but they didn't learn the lessons I might have hoped.

"Okay, let's try this again," I say. "Does anyone have an example of being called a name they *didn't like* being called?" I share my childhood nickname to connect with the kids staring at me without raising their hands.

"Kids in school used to call me 'ginger' because I have red hair. That used to really bother me because I didn't want to be known for the color of my hair. I wanted to be known for who I *was.*"

The room is dead silent, and I wait for volunteers.

Another moment passes by, and then I hear Jax's voice.

"People used to call me Brianna, and it really bothered me."

The class remains completely silent, and I'm unsure what to do with Jax's comment. Everyone turns to look at them as if to evaluate whether they look like a Brianna or a Jax.

I'm so glad that Jax felt comfortable enough to share something so personal, but I'm also worried about how their classmates will handle it. I'm unsure what to expect between Cody and his straightforward questions without any tact or sugarcoating and Oliver's insistence that he wasn't gay when I asked for his pronouns.

"Thanks for sharing," I finally say. "And now you go by Jax, right?" I clarify for the class.

Jax nods their head and adds, "and my pronouns are 'they' and 'them.'"

I'm impressed with Jax for openly declaring their preferred name and pronouns among *this* group of students.

"Awesome. Thanks, Jax."

I decide this is the perfect segue into our activity. I address the class, "I've been hearing students call a lot of things gay during class time, even though what they *mean* is something different entirely. Today we're going to look at what's so wrong about saying 'that's so gay.'" Several students roll their eyes, and Oliver lets a laugh escape.

I have posters around the room with the suggested questions from the Learning For Justice website. Giselle was kind enough to lend me butcher paper so I could do a gallery walk with the students. Each poster has a different question for students to consider. Students will walk around the room independently and write their anonymous answers on the posters with the corresponding questions. They may also use the opportunity to respond to other comments they see on the posters. It's an anonymous conversation that requires engagement from every student. I encourage them to take their time and respond to each poster.

After the students had ample time to contemplate the essential questions, I asked them to take a lap around the room and jot down some of the things they noticed about the responses. I told them to prepare to share at least one thing they noticed or learned with the class.

I wind the giant whiteboard timer (another first paycheck splurge) to 10 minutes, then release the students to write down their observations. I carefully watch the students to see their facial expressions while they read. Most are entirely expressionless. A few have looks of distaste, and a few look uncomfortable. The kids take their seats once everyone has written something and the timer goes off.

"Alright, great work, everyone. Let's talk about what we saw. That first question asked what you think of when you hear the word 'gay.' What stood out to you when you read the answers to the first question?"

"A lot of people said rainbows," one student offers. I nod in confirmation.

Another student adds, "I saw the word 'happy.'"

"Okay, how about the second question? In what ways have you heard the word 'gay' used? What did you notice about the answers?"

The students sit silently for a moment, looking at their papers, too afraid to venture an answer. I try to wait them out.

After a minute or two, Jax raises their hand again. I'm so impressed that they're brave enough to be the first ones to answer an uncomfortable discussion question. "I noticed the answers were mostly negative."

I nodded my head knowingly again. "Yeah, most often when I hear someone say 'that's gay,' it's meant to be an insult to make someone feel bad or less-than."

I wait for any other courageous students, but no one volunteers anything to add. "What about the next question? The question asked why you think some people use the phrase 'that's so gay.' Again, what did you notice about the answers?"

This time a few students raise their hands. They point out that perhaps people don't understand it's not a nice thing to say and that they probably mean they dislike something.

"The next question asks how *you* would feel if someone said 'that's so gay' about something you were doing or liked. What did you notice about the answers?"

Cody responds, "Miss, I wouldn't care. I know I'm not gay, and that's all that matters. And as long as I like what I'm doing, who cares what other people think?"

"Okay..." I'm trying to keep the conversation as impersonal and broad as possible since we aren't allowed to discuss gender identity or sexual orientation in class. "And what did you notice about the answers your classmates wrote?"

"A lot of people didn't care," he says.

"Some people said they'd be mad," Oliver adds.

I find it ironic that he volunteers this answer since he would be mad, gauging by our conversation during the first week of school.

"Why do you think some people would be mad about it?" I ask.

"Because they're not gay." His answer is quick, and his voice sounds defensive.

"Okay, if a phrase could possibly upset someone, can we agree as a class that we probably *shouldn't* use it?" Most students nod, and I say, "Okay, so we're in complete agreement that we will not use the phrase 'that's so gay.'" I put a thumbs-up in the air and raise my eyebrows, indicating I expect them to concur with me. Most students give me a thumbs up, and no one gives me a thumbs down, so I hand out their final assignment.

The culmination of the activity has students work together to create a poster, pamphlet, or even just a letter to the school newspaper explaining why it's not appropriate to call things 'gay' when we don't like them. Most students seem more than happy to start the activity, and the rest are excited to talk to their peers for the rest of the period.

I had hoped I would have been able to have some life-changing conversation with them where every single one of them would become lifelong LGBTQ+ allies and advocates, but that just isn't realistic. Realistically, each of these kids comes from different backgrounds. I don't know which of them are even allowed to discuss LGBTQ+ stuff at home. I don't want to create controversy; I just want to create a safe and equitable learning environment to the best of my ability.

Every kid deserves that.

The lesson went fine the rest of the day. Students mainly chose not to speak or participate. I can understand why they might not want to participate and speak up. Being the first to do something completely counter to the rest of your peers or society is always hard. It seems like if the majority of the students are supportive and kind, the ones that aren't stay quiet.

At the end of the day, a group of students stop by to say hello and kill time. I'm probably way more excited about this than I should be, but it's the first time students have just casually stopped by.

The group consists of Jax from my first-period English class, Sabrina from my 7th-period honors class, and a student I've never met. The three of them are laughing about something when they walk in, and it's the first time I've seen Jax with friends. I'm so, so glad to see they *have* friends.

Still working on my lesson for the rest of the week, I'm sitting at my desk at the front of the room when they enter. Jax, today wearing a Metallica t-shirt and plaid pants with… beat-up old Chucks… escorts the unknown student to my desk.

"Miss!" Jax says excitedly. "I wanted to introduce you to my friend Erin. I've been telling them all about your class and how awesome you are."

My face completely lights up, and I feel this incredible warmth spread through my whole body. "Aww, thanks, Jax. You're super awesome too."

"So Erin is the president of the Pride Alliance Club here on campus."

I wonder how long that will be a thing with the new policies in place. I wonder how long it will be before they start preventing students from discussing their real lives on campus.

"Well, it's very nice to meet you, Erin. Are you a freshman also?"

"No, no, no. I'm a junior."

"Miss, I just wanted to say thank you for doing that lesson today," Jax interjects. "I know some kids still don't get it, but it meant a lot to have a teacher stick up for that. For us."

"Of course, Jax. Not only is it common decency, but this is also a publicly funded education system. Every student deserves to feel safe and welcome here. My job is to make sure that's true."

My eyes shift back to Jax's outfit, and I notice again the plaid pants and old, worn Chuck Taylors.

Suddenly, I'm 12 years old again, and Stacy and I were walking home from school with our arms linked. We're singing AJR's "100 Bad Days" and heading to our usual pit stop at the corner gas station for the regular Takis and Mountain Dew before heading back to my house. Stacy would spend as much time as she could at my house, only going home when she absolutely had to.

Jax starts to tilt their head a little and raise their eyebrows, their nose bridge piercing rising with it. I mimic their facial expression and realize they've asked me a question.

"Oh, uh… yes. Sure, I'd love to come to check out a Pride Alliance Club meeting. When do you guys meet?"

"Wednesdays at lunch in Ms. Hawkins' room. We could use another advisor for when she's out. And students can always use more allies," Erin finishes.

I'm so thrilled right now. I feel like I made a difference. I feel like I impacted a student positively beyond academics—my whole mission as a teacher. This feels better than double-star days at Starbucks.

"Woo hoo! See you Wednesday then!" Jax shouts.

I can't stop smiling and give a little wave of goodbye as they walk out. Once they've left, I spend the next hour integrating multiple educational applications across different platforms for the upcoming lessons Penny has designed.

After finishing up and gathering all my things, I stopped by my whiteboard to change the date and write the agenda on the board for tomorrow. It's become my habit before leaving the next day; otherwise, it doesn't get done.

When I pick up a dry erase marker, I notice something is already written on the agenda. Well, doodled, really. In the space for the agenda was a big heart that said inside: *WE LOVE MS. WHITE.* I'm flooded with joy and probably glowing as I walk to the parking lot.

When I finally make it home and through the door of my parent's house, I drop my teaching bag by the front door and head to the kitchen for a glass of wine to celebrate. I pull the cork out of the already opened bottle, and enjoy the sound and smell of the Riesling as it pours into my favorite wine glass. I head into my bedroom, plop down on my chair that feels like a hug, and turn on the TV.

While scanning through the movie selections, I hear my phone ping. Picking it up from the nightstand beside me, I notice an email in my inbox from the principal, Mr. Sanders. I open my mail app and read:

Ms. White,

Please plan on meeting with me after school tomorrow. We've had a parent complaint that we need to address with you.

I run through the lesson in my head and wonder what part of it could have made a student uncomfortable and what could have gotten back to parents before the school day even ended.

I think about Jax mentioning their former name and current pronouns during the first period, but surely that couldn't have upset anyone. Jax never talked about their gender identity; we never discussed anything about their gender identity or anyone else's...

And then, I try to imagine which student could have been upset by the incident. I wonder if it could have been Oliver, but I did the lesson four times. It could have been any student from any period.

All that joy and happiness from the success of today has been replaced by fear and dread. My stomach is in knots, so I decide to toss my phone on the bed next to me—just out of reach— and focus on my wine and the next biography I've been waiting to read: *The Mayor of Castro Street: The Life and Times of Harvey Milk.*

Harvey Milk was the first openly gay politician in San Francisco, but he was murdered less than a year after taking his position as City Supervisor. I thought that reading about him might help me understand how we got where we are now regarding LGBTQ+ rights and laws.

During the summer, I listened to a podcast about a serial killer named John Gacy. He was essentially so ashamed of being gay that he would pick up men to sleep with and then kill them. He was also a psychopath, but the fact that he was ashamed of his sexuality and sought men to murder still stands.

So how did a gay mayor hold office during that same time period? How did we get from a gay mayor to students not being allowed to even acknowledge their gay parents while at school? I take a long sip of wine and open the book to find out.

15

Thursday morning, I woke up with a terrible headache. Apparently, two glasses of wine without dinner wasn't the best idea. Before hopping in the shower, I pop two Advil and down a bottle of water. I don't think about the meeting I have with Mr. Sanders at the end of the day, or I might throw up—whether from the wine or the nerves, I'm not sure. But I make a mental note to myself to avoid wine on weeknights from here on out.

Once I'm done showering, and the pounding in my head has dulled slightly, I dig through my closet for something to wear. I know I will be reprimanded today, so I feel like I should look a little extra professional to show that I care about my job. Instead of another patterned dress, I chose sensible black slacks and a solid light blue button-up shirt. My teaching wardrobe is scarce, but I try to buy a staple item with each paycheck. I hope this outfit will give the impression that I care greatly about my job and wish to remain employed. I finish by pulling my frizzy red hair into a respectable braid.

My stomach is in absolute knots, but I grab a bagel and a cup of coffee for the drive to work just in case. For the entire

25-minute drive, I'm catastrophizing about the meeting. Maybe Mr. Sanders will have to fire me. I suppose with the national teacher shortage, I still might be able to find a job somewhere. Districts hire teachers that are fired for parent complaints, right?

When I finally get to school and make it to my classroom, Jax is waiting outside my door.

"Jax! What's up?" I ask curiously.

"Nothing, Miss. I wanted to say thank you again for doing that lesson yesterday. Some of the kids in that class say really mean stuff when you're not around."

"Oh, really?" I ask. I can't imagine students saying mean stuff without the teacher realizing it. Without *me* noticing it.

"Yeah, like Cody and Oliver. They're always making fun of people and keep calling each other the 'F' word. It makes me uncomfortable."

"The 'F' word?" I ask.

"F-A-G," Jax spells out.

"Oooh." I nod my head. I feel terrible that I hadn't caught it before.

"Yeah. So maybe they won't do that anymore," they add.

"Well, next time they do it, let me know," I say. "I'll put an end to it right then and there."

"Okay. Thanks again, Miss," Jax says and walks away.

I enter my classroom and ruminate on our conversation. If kids call each other derogatory names without me knowing, what else is happening that I don't see? And if Jax has thanked me *twice* for the lesson I did on calling things gay, maybe it's worth the parent complaint and reprimand.

When lunch arrives that day, I decide I should seek guidance from anyone willing. I make my way to Penny's room and knock on the door. I don't see her sitting at her desk through the tiny window, but that doesn't mean she isn't in her room.

I decide to wait a few minutes longer because I really have

no idea what I'm walking into later today. And while I'm thinking about that, Penny's door swings open, startling me.

"Sam!" she shouts happily. "What can I do for you?" I love how peppy Penny is. Right now, pep and encouragement are exactly what I need.

"I was wondering if I could chat with you for a moment?" I ask hesitantly.

"Absolutely. Come on in."

I follow Penny into her room and sit at one of the desks. Penny sits at her desk and rummages around in the drawers for something, distracted.

"I have a meeting with Mr. Sanders after school today about a lesson I did. I guess there was a parent complaint." I wonder if Penny can hear my voice shaking. I'm trying not to cry, but my anxiety makes that near impossible.

"Oh, what was the lesson?" She asks, no longer digging through her desk.

"It was about why it's not okay to call things gay as an insult."

She purses her lips and moves her mouth around like some cartoon character while she's thinking.

"Okay, so Mr. Sanders and Mrs. Morris will probably both be in the meeting. They'll ask about the lesson, tell you the parent's complaint, and then you'll probably just need to contact the parent to make amends. No big deal." She sounds so... unperturbed. For someone who lobbied for these new policies to pass, I certainly expected her to be more shocked about my lesson. In fact, I figured that meeting with her would be an excellent precursor to prepare me for whatever happens after school today. Instead, it just feels like a waste of time.

"Who's Mrs. Morris?" I ask. Although I've been here since August, I still don't know the names of all the administrators. The campus is just too big.

"Mrs. Morris is your evaluator. She's the admin over the English department this year. In fact, you should have already had your first observation and pre-evaluation conference with her."

My stomach drops again, and I wonder if my stomach even has a bottom. My heart rate is speeding up.

"I haven't even met her," I say.

"Well, good thing you have a meeting after school today," she responds. Somehow, meeting with Penny has made me feel worse, not better.

"Well, thanks for the talk. I have to get back to my room before my Hot Pocket gets cold."

She waves bye, and I leave her room. Instead of heading directly to mine, I head to Emma Holland's room. She's been incredibly friendly and might have solid advice for me on how to handle the situation I'm about to encounter.

When I get to Emma's room, her door is already propped open. I knock casually before entering the room.

"Hey, Emma. I was wondering if I could get some advice from you about something," My voice is noticeably shaking now.

"Yeah, of course," she says with concern. "Is everything okay? You look like you're about to cry."

And with that, the floodgates open, and the waterworks begin. I start crying and immediately bring my hands to cover my embarrassment.

"Sam, what's going on?" she asks again.

"A parent complained about a lesson I did yesterday," I say through broken sobs. "Now I have to meet with Mr. Sanders and Mrs. Morris. Apparently, she's the supervisor for our department, and I should have had my first evaluation with her already. Basically, I think I'm going to get fired today, and I'm kind of freaking out."

I continue to cry, and Emma walks over and hands me a box of tissues.

"Okay, well, first off, let's address the evaluation. It's *her* job to make sure you get evaluated—not yours. If you're worried, email her and ask when your first evaluation will be. Or, you can do what I do and not worry about it."

"Not worry about it?" I ask.

"Definitely not worry about it. Evaluations must be done by certain deadlines, and the admin is the only person responsible for those deadlines. You can't get in trouble for someone *else* not doing their job."

I nod in understanding but can't seem to stop the stream of tears regardless.

"So tell me about the lesson. What was it? What do you think a parent might have complained about?"

"Okay, so I had all these kids calling each other gay, so I did a lesson on why that's not okay. I even had a nonbinary student come to me after school yesterday and again today to thank me for doing the lesson. But a parent complained, possibly because I used the word gay, and now I don't know what to do."

"A lesson on the word gay, huh?" she clarifies.

"Yes. But I didn't ever define the word, talk about gender identity, or talk about gay people. We literally only focused on the use of the word, what people mean when they use it, and why it's not okay to use it as a derogatory term." I'm out of breath when I finish trying to get the words out so quickly. I desperately want to explain myself. I desperately want to remain employed. What other job would I be able to use those 15 stacking paper trays I bought?

"Okay, here's what you're going to do. You're going to get a union representative to go with you to the meeting, so you have a witness. Then, you're going to explain to Mr. Sanders and Mrs. Morris exactly what you just explained to me—you were doing a lesson to mitigate potential bullying that might occur. You had your students' best interest at heart."

"I *did* have my students' best interest at heart! That was the whole reason I did the lesson!" I say emphatically.

"Okay, so at the end of the day, that's what matters. You have a solid reason for teaching the lesson, it sounds like you didn't make the lesson about anything LGBTQ+ related per se, and you had students thank you. It sounds like your reasoning is solid. I'm sure you have nothing to worry about." She gives me a reassuring smile.

The bell rings, startling both of us. My tears have finally subsided, so I wipe my face and throw away the tissues. Emma walks with me to her door to greet incoming students.

"Thank you for the reassurance," I say quietly.

"Sam, you've got a good heart. You're a good teacher. Someday, you'll be a great teacher. Don't let the bastards grind you down."

A wide smile covers my face now as I remember the iconic saying. In The *Handmaid's Tale*, Atwood's protagonist Offred uses this phrase for inspiration. It helps her fight, and it helps her stay alive.

Don't let the bastards grind me down, I repeat to myself while returning to my classroom.

After the last bell of the day, Sabrina stays behind in my classroom to fangirl over the Hamilton musical. I hate having to kick her out of the room, but I know showing up late to this meeting isn't going to help my case. I tell her I have a parent-teacher conference and promise her we will gush over John Laurens' character next time I see her.

I take my laptop, a notebook, and a pen to take notes. I figure I may need to show my research. As I walk to the meeting, several students shout "Hi, Miss!" and smile as I pass. I used to think it was odd that students didn't use my name, but now I've gotten used to it.

When I arrive in the office, Amy, Mr. Sanders' secretary, is telling a student they can have their confiscated cell phone when their guardian shows up to retrieve it.

The angry student responds with, "Bitch, bye," and stomps off.

My eyes widen in shock. Amy notices me and laughs at my expression.

"Don't worry," she says. "She doesn't realize I get to have

a conversation with her parents when they pick up her phone. Also, she's on the basketball team. Her coach will have her doing laps for days."

"Ha… that's funny," I say, mustering up as much enthusiasm as possible.

"I'll let Mr. Sanders know you're here. Don't be nervous," she adds before picking up the phone to dial his extension.

"Ms. White is here for your meeting," she says pleasantly. After another second, she hangs up and says, "You can go in."

She smiles reassuringly at me again, and I smile back at her. I walk behind her desk and open Mr. Sander's office door. I'm painfully aware that I don't have a union representative with me as Emma suggested, but I'm not yet a union member.

The office is bigger than I could have imagined. It even has its own bathroom, and I'm instantly jealous. How much time could I save daily by having a bathroom attached to my classroom?

"Good afternoon, Ms. White. Come on in and have a seat," he says, gesturing to the two chairs opposite him.

I take a seat and let my eyes explore the room. I'm surprised that he has almost no decorations or personal effects. There is one small frame next to the computer with a picture of his family, but that's it. Nothing else around the room gives me clues about his personality or how to make the best impression. I cross my legs and fold my hands in my lap to try and seem calm.

"How's it going?" he asks. I wish he would skip the small talk. I just want to apologize, grovel, and get this over with.

"It's going okay," I respond. "It would be better if a parent hadn't complained, but otherwise, it's going alright."

"Yes, yes. How is your honor's class going?"

I'm slightly confused by the question but quickly realize that's probably the class period the complaint came from, which is odd because it's the last period of the day. I received the email almost immediately after school.

"It's going fine, I think. Some of the students are really

struggling with the content, but I think it's going well overall," I answer.

"And how is Monica Ruiz doing in that class?"

My eyebrows go up, and I hesitantly respond, "Well, she's actually one of the ones struggling."

"Did you know that her dad is on the school board?"

I did *not* know her dad was on the school board.

"Really?" I ask, surprised.

"And Mrs. Juarez is her aunt."

Penny Juarez, my department chair, is Monica Ruiz's aunt. Oh shit. My face begins to redden with the realization.

"I definitely didn't know that," I say sheepishly.

"I didn't think so, which is why I wanted this meeting. Anything that happens in your classroom *will* get back to Mrs. Juarez and Mr. Ruiz. I know you're a first-year teacher, so I wanted to give you a little bit of… a heads up about what that might look like for you."

I nod slowly in disbelief.

"I also wanted to make you aware that it was mostly Mr. Ruiz and Mrs. Juarez lobbying for the new laws and policies. Well, they were the face of the 'movement' anyway. This is their passion project."

I nod knowingly. This explains a lot. This is probably why Penny didn't seem surprised when I told her about this meeting. She already knew. This also explains why her advice was so… cavalier.

"That's good to know. Thank you," I say. "What was the complaint about?"

"The word 'gay' being used in a lesson."

"Just the word being used?" I ask.

"Just the word. The whole lesson was about the word. Well, that and the fact that it wasn't in the lesson plans online available for community viewing. Listen, I'm not upset, and you're not in trouble. I just want you to be aware that you will get a lot of pushback if you continue down this road."

Down what road? I wonder. *The road of supporting teens and*

LGBTQ+ youth?

And really, what am I supposed to do when students make these gay comments? I have to protect *those* kids. We're protecting the kids who don't want to know about the existence of the LGBTQ+ community or want to wipe out the community entirely—so who's protecting the LGBTQ+ kids? Pushback or not, I think this is a road worth going down.

"Alright, Ms. White. That will be all."

"Thank you, Mr. Sanders," I say while standing up. I walk out of the office and close the door, puzzling over what just happened.

I make a mental note to write down Monica's family connections on the seating chart, so I don't forget. What other surprises are in store for me this year?

16

By December, I've finally managed to make my way to a Pride Alliance club meeting. Erin, the president, is standing in front of an impressive Promethean smart board jotting down notes for the agenda when I walk in. Giselle is at her desk, grading papers, and I sit near her.

She looks up at me and smiles. "Welcome to our cult," she says jokingly.

"Oooh, tell me more!" I whisper conspiratorially. She waves me to a chair behind her desk, and I take a seat. I never cared too much for gossip in high school and didn't have friends that gossiped in college. Now that I'm a teacher, I can't seem to get away from it. And I can't say that I entirely mind. It seems to be the only way to learn anything about anything. How else would I know about the principal's expectations for my classroom?

"The Shipman Republicans Club and the kids from the Christian Club don't get along with the kids from Pride Alliance," Giselle shares. "It's a friendly rivalry for the most part—just clubs competing against each other. But some kids made a joke about Pride Alliance being like a cult because everyone is so close. They decided to run with it and refer to themselves as the Pride Alliance Cult."

"Clever," I say.

"And resilient," she adds. "These kids have to be with what they're up against in school."

"Tell me more," I urge her. I haven't talked to her since before my meeting with Mr. Sanders, so I'm curious about her take on the experience of LGBTQ+ students on our campus.

"Well, they're constantly dealing with anti-LGBTQ language. I hear kids call each other gay at least a few times daily. Not in my classes, of course. Well, that's not entirely true. I hear it, but kids *immediately* apologize so they won't have to hear one of my lectures."

Her students are conscious of their language in her class. That's cool. I wonder how we get them to stop saying it altogether, though. Or get them to stop associating things that are "lesser" with "gay."

"But honestly, so many of my students have rough situations at school or home because of their gender identity or sexual orientation. Half of these kids' parents don't even know they're part of the LGBTQ+ community. Erin—that's not even the name they use with their parent. When I call home for anything, I have to use a different name and pronoun. I even have some students with same-sex parents who aren't comfortable coming on campus. So, these kids *have to* be resilient to get through high school."

I'm somewhat shocked, but in all honesty… I don't know anything about the experience of LGBTQ+ students on my high school campus growing up. In fact, I never even met anyone from the community while I was in high school. Granted, I was timid due to my social anxiety and the potential for massive panic attacks when interacting with my peers. Still, how could I have not noticed… anyone?

"Wow. So how's it going with the new policies on campus? I can't believe we're allowed to even have this club anymore."

"Well," she responds, "the beauty is that it happens during lunch—which is 'duty-free' for teachers."

"Duty-free?" I ask.

"It means our contract specifically states we do not have to do anything work-related during our lunch breaks. Often times elementary school teachers have to do lunch duty or bus duty. We don't have much of that at the high school level, but the fact that it's in our contract means I can use this time however I want. And since it's not academic time, I can discuss whatever I want with the students."

"Sounds like I should read our contract," I say.

She laughs and responds, "Honestly, a decade into teaching, and I've never read one of my actual teaching contracts."

"Oh, thank god," I say with exaggerated relief. "I don't think I can handle trying to shove any more information in my head right now."

"School year's going that well for ya, huh?" she asks with raised eyebrows.

I sigh and confide, "It's been rough. I didn't expect these new policies, for one thing."

"I guess you haven't been following the national news over the last year. This district has been in the news constantly. In fact, we even had to have racial sensitivity training a few years back."

"What is *that*?" I ask, more concerned than curious.

"Basically, too many students and staff were openly racist on social media, so the district required us to do an intensive racial sensitivity training. I don't think it made much difference, but at least they did *something*."

"Wow," I say, reflecting on whether or not I've heard racist language from students or staff this year. I'm sure I have listened to many micro-aggressions, but nothing specific stands out in my mind.

"So, is it just the policies that are challenging for you right now?" she asks. She has an almost maternal feel about her.

She's only 10 or 15 years older than me, but something about her... aura... is just calming. And caring. She's just very mom-like.

"I wish it were just the policies. But it's not. I'm planning lessons until 7 or 8 every night, grading until around ten every night, subbing classes during my planning periods, and I just got reprimanded for doing a lesson on the phrase 'that's so gay.' I'm so overwhelmed with the workload and the anti-LGBTQ+ sentiments on campus." I know my whining is probably incredibly unprofessional, but I don't have the energy to care right now.

I'm seriously on the verge of tears. Crying at my first Pride Alliance meeting isn't exactly what I was going for, so I clear my throat, take a slow, deep breath in, and exhale even more slowly.

Giselle's face transforms into one of mild pity. "That's really rough. I'm sorry, Sam. If you ever need someone to vent to, I'm here. I promise anything you say will stay between us, and I'm happy to give you any tiny amount of guidance that I might be able to offer."

I give her a tight smile in response. I don't want to be the whiny teacher always complaining about stuff, so I end my rant there.

"Well, I think you'll enjoy the club meeting today. We've got some good stuff on the agenda." The expression she gives me is hopeful but still conveys plenty of pity.

"Hello, everyone. We're gonna start the meeting, so take a seat and stop talking." Erin is poised and confident. Their smart-looking wire-framed glasses make them look like they are all business. Erin commands attention with their presence, and it's pretty impressive.

"The first thing on our agenda today is to discuss the prom court."

"Prom court is bullshit!" I hear a familiar voice shout. I

look towards the door to see Jax walking in. They scan the room, and when their eyes land on me, their whole face lights up.

"Ms. White! You finally came!"

"That's me," I say unenthusiastically. I hate when attention is called to me. Unless I'm the teacher, I want to be invisible in most situations. I don't know why teaching is the exception, but it is.

Jax walks over to an empty desk and sits beside a few friends. Today, Jax has their mohawk back and what's left of their shaved hair on their head is dyed orange. Jax is wearing ridiculously ripped jeans and a shirt I haven't seen before that says, "PRIDE IS A PROTEST." Their wardrobe absolutely fascinates me.

"Prom court *is* bullshit because it's always a king and queen, male and female," Jax begins. "Where does that leave the Shipman students who don't identify as male or female? Does a non-binary student have to choose a gender to participate? They have to choose one of *two* limiting gender assignments if they want to play any sports or use a bathroom here on campus. Prom court *is* bullshit."

"Yeah!" a random student shouts their agreement from somewhere in the packed classroom. Several other students hoot and holler in support of Erin's declaration.

"So, what are we going to do about it?" Erin asks the group. "This is why we're here—to make changes. How can we change prom court to be more inclusive? Give me all your good, great, terrible, and awful ideas."

Students start volunteering suggestions or making jokes, and Erin jots down the comments on the Promethean board.

"Let's get rid of the titles," someone suggests. "That seems like the first step."

"Yeah," Jax interjects, "Let's just call them 'royalty' or 'prom court.'" Students seem to agree as multiple heads nod up and down, and a broad smile covers Jax's face. You can tell they are proud of participating, and I'm proud of them too.

Anytime someone with anxiety participates, it feels like a small win for anxiety sufferers everywhere.

The students continue to share ideas as Erin furiously tries to write it all down. Some students suggest Shipman High gets rid of prom altogether, followed by a lot of booing. One student suggests seniors nominate the prom court—with no gender requirements. The two seniors with the most votes win prom royalty. I'm really impressed with their ability to have a productive conversation about something serious during their lunch period.

"Alright, I'm going to need someone to draft a proposal, and we'll need everyone's help to collect signatures. Who will write the proposal?" Erin is all business, and at least half of the packed classrooms of students are maintaining focus.

Jax raises their hand to volunteer to write the proposal, and I'm again surprised. For someone with anxiety, Jax is getting a lot of attention and handling it marvelously. I'm really proud. In high school, my anxiety wasn't under control enough to participate in class activities. I would often ditch on days we had to do group work. Luckily, I was also a nerd, so I still graduated with an impressive GPA.

"Great!" Erin exclaims. "Then we need some signature pages and clipboards. Ms. Hawkins, can you take care of those items for us?"

"You got it," Giselle says, jotting Erin's requests on a bright neon pink post-it.

"Alright, everyone. Our last order of business is the 'Day of Silence.' This year, it's going to be on April 2nd, so we want to make sure everyone knows about it in advance. It's the last day before Spring Break, so I'm not sure how many students will participate. We're going to make posters for the event after school on Friday here in Ms. Hawkins' room. Please show up to help if you can!"

With that, the bell rings, and students begin to clean up their messes and gather their belongings for the last period of the day.

"That was really awesome," I tell Giselle. "I'm super impressed with how poised and focused Erin was. I've never seen a teenager run a meeting of a group of teenagers, so… well."

"Yes, Erin is amazing. They were the first agender student I ever met. I remember when they came up and told me after class one day, I had to have Erin explain what it even meant."

"Wow. It sounds like Erin is pretty mature for their age," I comment.

"Oh, they are for sure. And they're doing amazing stuff with the club. They became president last year as a sophomore because they're *that* impressive. You should come to more meetings."

"I would really love to," I say honestly, though I have no idea how I'll fit it in or manage to heat my forlorn Hot Pocket in the teacher's lounge *and* find my way back to Giselle's room with enough time to eat my food and be present for the meeting. "I'm not sure if I can make it work, but I'm definitely going to try."

Giselle smiles and says, "Good! These are awesome kids, and they could use another ally."

She stands to start prepping for her last period, and I stand to head back to my classroom.

17

Since we rotate classrooms for each Professional Learning Community meeting, the next meeting is in Emma Holland's classroom. Emma's classroom is a lot like her; organized and extremely put-together. It's already November, and I still haven't seen Emma wear anything besides high heels, perfect hair, and no makeup. I've also never seen her have a bad day, an unpleasant disposition, or even a hint of the stress I've been feeling all semester.

Her room is very minimalist. There is a sign with the class expectations, but the rest of the walls are bare. She has labeled bins for each class period's assignments and—more interestingly—her desks are in straight rows.

As usual, I'm the first one at the meeting. I enter and take a seat at the back of the room.

"I really like your desks," I say.

"Yeah, me too," she responds with a sort of conspiratorial smile.

"You don't get in trouble for having rows instead of groups?" I ask. I absolutely loathe groups. I can't get students to keep their eyes on me or focus on their work. On top of that, they won't stop talking and messing with each other. Also, sitting in groups seems to somehow require immediate paper football participation. It's a nightmare.

"Are you kidding? No one has been in my classroom even once this year. Who's going to know?" She's still smiling and seems completely unfazed. I need to know her secret to being so… *cool*.

I think back over the last few months and realize that no one has been in my room either. Penny hasn't even stopped by. She commented about my desks and Emma's right—how would anyone ever know?

"I've been having such a hard time with groups," I confide. "I can't get the kids to pay attention to *me* instead of the person they're facing—and that's for the students who *aren't* looking at their phones."

"Switch it up! Change them to rows! If anyone says anything, say that it's for attendance purposes and the students put them in groups later."

Really, Emma? It's that easy? It took me almost an entire semester to learn this trick, and I'm both thrilled and frustrated. I'm thrilled because, dear God, I cannot take any more of these groups. I'm frustrated because It's November. That's three and a half months of small group hell that I could have avoided.

How do people figure it out? How do people know when it's okay to try to circumvent the rules and when it isn't? How do you know that rearranging desks is one of the things you can get away with? I guess that's why I should spend more time with veteran teachers.

"How are you feeling about the new policies?" I ask.

"Who cares? I'm going to teach whatever I want because there's nobody in my room. I typically avoid conversations about most of the stuff in the new policies anyway, so that helps. How's your planning going?"

I think carefully about how to answer that question. I want to sound capable and professional, but I also really need help. I spend hours each week preparing lessons for my classes, and I'm burnt out. My one prep period a day isn't enough time to create materials from scratch, grade, and plan for future lessons—especially when I have to document supplemental materials so far in advance and get approval for them. I'm overwhelmed and starting to feel like I'm drowning. I was using Penny's lesson plans, but she stopped posting her slide decks and materials with her lesson plans, so I can't copy them as easily anymore.

"Honestly, it's a struggle. There aren't enough hours in the day to get all the planning done," I respond.

"Have you checked out CommonLit.org?"

I shake my head no, and she tells me about the website. She tells me about the free unit plans with pre-made worksheets, quizzes, rubrics, and slide decks. It sounds like a godsend.

Emma is still rattling away about the website when Diogo and Giselle walk in together. Diogo is wearing khaki pants and a t-shirt with a ukulele-strumming sloth that says *Meditation is my jam!* Suddenly, I hear Justin Bieber singing in my head, "*If I was your boyfriend, never let you go...*" I think I can smell a hint of saltwater while I picture the imaginary ocean breeze blowing through his hair...

The classroom door slams behind Penny, and I'm back in Emma's classroom. Penny immediately goes to the front of the room to take her rightful place as PLC lead.

Everyone sits at a desk in the front row, and Penny starts the meeting.

" I want to respect everyone's time by starting and ending on time. So we have a few things to go over. First, let's talk about lesson plans. We absolutely *cannot* teach a lesson that hasn't been available for community review for at least two weeks."

I can feel my face immediately begin to burn red in

embarrassment. I'm sure she's referring to my recent off-script lesson. Admin probably told her she needed to remind everyone since I couldn't seem to remember.

Emma's hand goes up and says, "Uh, what if I realize my students don't know something they should? Do I need to teach a foundational lesson for the planned lesson?"

Penny doesn't look pleased, but her facial expression is only slightly annoyed.

"Well..." Penny's voice trails off, and I can tell she's thinking hard about her answer. She can't very well say *not* to teach the foundational piece that's necessary... can she? After another silent moment, she finally sighs deeply and says, "That's why we use pre-assessments. Everyone should be using pre-assessments for every unit."

She looks satisfied with her answer and gives an additional nod as if to punctuate her response.

We're supposed to be using pre-assessments? I'm so glad I found out before the school year ended...

Emma's hand goes up again, and she doesn't wait for Penny to acknowledge her before saying, "And what about when we get new students? It's November, and I've gotten five new students this month *alone*. Do I just assume they have the same foundational knowledge as their peers?"

"Obviously, there will have to be some wiggle room for things like that."

"Actually, there's nothing obvious about it," Emma retorts. "The amount of micromanaging is ridiculous. The students are the ones that suffer."

"Well, you're welcome to bring it up at a board meeting, Emma."

Penny seems to have lost some of her pep and composure, and I'm getting a little uncomfortable.

"I'm not interested in dealing with it at the district level. I understand these are site-based decisions, and I think there should have been more discussion on the repercussions for faculty, staff, *and* students."

"Well, Ms. Holland, unfortunately, that's not your decision," Penny says.

"No shit. If I were a department chair, I would never let these insane policies pass. I would stand up for my teachers and trust their professionalism. I would trust that their degrees and ability to get hired make them qualified to teach."

The tension in the room is palpable, and Penny's voice begins to rise.

"For goodness sake, Emma! This is the first year in a decade that we haven't had to all teach the *exact* same thing at all times. That's what *you* wanted. You have to give a little to get a little. I realize you're unhappy, but you will have to make peace with these policies. It is what it is, and I'm the department chair for the next year and a half." Penny's face is red, and she seems out of breath from talking so fast.

She's obviously angry, and Emma apparently decides to concede because she lifts both hands in the air as if to surrender. Penny takes a moment to sip her water before continuing the meeting.

"Now, as I was saying, if a lesson hasn't been available for community review for a *minimum* of two weeks before being taught, you cannot teach the lesson. Parents have a right to know *exactly* what their children are taught."

"We're not allowed to use leftover class time to teach *anything* extra. No bell-to-bell instruction. Duly noted..." Emma mumbles to herself. Luckily, her mumbling is loud enough for all of us to hear. She doesn't look up when she murmurs, so nobody responds to her comment.

"The next thing on the agenda is the supplemental text reviews. After careful consideration, the administration team and department chairs have decided there needs to be a more stringent set of guidelines for the supplemental texts with a more extended period for previewing materials.

"As a result, we've decided we will not *use* supplemental texts this semester. All supplemental texts you wished to be used for the second semester must be submitted by December

1st.”

I look around the room at my colleague's reactions. Giselle's jaw has nearly dropped to the floor, and her face is one of anger and appall. Emma has a slight smirk on her face that I can't reasonably interpret. Diogo has a similar look to Giselle's, but one more of astonishment than anger.

"What about all our lesson plans we've already created for this semester with supplemental texts? Or... around supplemental texts? How are we supposed to stick to textbooks from the district when we don't even *have* textbooks?" Giselle demands.

"I understand your frustration, Ms. Hawkins," Penny begins.

"After four years, I think you can start calling me Giselle," Giselle interjects.

With an irritated sigh, Penny continues, "but this is the decision Mr. Sanders has made, so this is what we're doing."

Giselle's tirade seems to be just beginning. She stands up from her desk and says, "This is absurd. I'm sorry, but it is. How is it possible that we are given a dozen or so novels to choose from but no other curriculum support other than mandatory trainings and lesson plan submissions? And neither of those provide actual teaching-content support. So the district says, 'Choose one of these available books, figure out how to get the students equal access, and then create all the materials from scratch with zero planning time.'"

"Correct," Penny says matter-of-factly, then continues with her announcement. "Because of the sheer volume of supplemental texts, we're going to form a committee. One teacher from each grade level will volunteer to join the committee and review the supplemental text lists together. The committee will be responsible for approving or denying materials, and only approved materials may be used."

I glance to the left and look over at Giselle. She has finally sat back down but sits on the edge of her seat. The tension in here is incredibly uncomfortable. I wonder if any of my other colleagues are feeling it. Giselle seems very involved with her cell phone now, and Diogo is smiling at Penny.

"And finally, this is a friendly reminder not to discuss mental health issues with students in the classroom. This seems to be something some of our Shipman teachers are struggling with, so Mr. Sanders would like the department chairs to reiterate it to everyone."

I think back carefully over the last several weeks and wonder if I've spoken to any students about their mental health. I've been learning a lot about their mental health from the Soundtrack of Your Life paragraphs, but I haven't actually spoken to any students about their mental health.

I also haven't seen or heard of any students trying to talk to their teachers about mental health stuff. I wonder if they know about the new policies or somehow sense their teachers distancing themselves.

This time, it's Giselle's hand that goes up. "So you're effectively saying we can't say to students, 'Good morning; how are you?'"

"Of course, you can say good morning to students, Giselle." Penny is starting to sound exasperated. I wonder how other PLC's are handling the new policies and myriad of disgruntled teachers.

"Well," Giselle continues, "If I ask a student how they're doing and they tell me honestly, that's discussing their mental health."

"The policy refers to stuff about depression, anxiety, suicide, and sexual orientation, Giselle. You need to understand the spirit of the policies and why they were adopted."

"No," she counters. "I need to understand how to implement them in my classroom when they're completely counterintuitive. I need to understand which research-based teaching methods—such as building student relationships—I should ignore to comply with your policies."

"They're not *my* policies," Penny says defensively. Her

voice is starting to rise a bit again, and this seems personal now.

"*You* did the leg work to get them passed and implemented. These are *your* policies. These do not represent the majority of our students or staff. These policies don't protect our students and staff. So, again, I ask—to what degree do I ignore students if they try to tell me about their mental health?"

"It seems like you're being adversarial for the sake of being adversarial. If you're unsure, Giselle, just stop the conversation and fill out a Google Form for the student's counselor. They will follow up with the student."

"Okay, so once I submit that form to the counselor, my mandated reporter obligations have been filled?" She sounds incredibly aggressive, and I realize managing her emotions might not be one of her strongest skills.

Penny scrunches up her face to think for a minute. It seems she didn't consider the mandated reporter role teachers also play. As teachers, we are legally required to report to admin and Child Protective Services if we hear of a student being hurt, see that they've been hurt, or believe they might hurt themselves or someone else. If a teacher doesn't report something and it comes out that they were aware of the issue in advance, that teacher is looking at a fine, jail time, and even losing their teaching license. It's pretty serious stuff.

"No, Giselle, go report it to admin if it falls into the mandated reporter category," Penny responds.

"Okay, just checking...." Giselle's voice trails off, and she scribbles something on the notepad next to her.

"Alright, I guess that's everything I had. Do you guys have any questions or concerns for me?"

Diogo raises his hand and says, "Yeah, I have a question. When are final exams due?"

Final exams? In November? I'm simultaneously confused and concerned. I hadn't even thought about final exams!

"You need to have your final exams emailed to admin for

approval no later than November 25th," Penny responds.

Everyone jots down the information furiously. Today is November 15th, leaving me only ten days to create an entire final exam and submit it to admin.

"Okay, dismissed everyone. Giselle, can I speak to you alone for a moment?" Penny asks.

Giselle nods and remains seated. I continue packing up my stuff to quell my curiosity.

Penny walks over and sits at the desk next to Giselle. "Alright, we had a community complaint about your lesson for next week."

"Which one?"

"The one where you ask students to analyze a bill regarding inclusive curriculum and then write about whether the new policies are in accordance with it," she says matter-of-factly. She doesn't even hesitate, and she isn't smiling. Peppy Penny doesn't seem so peppy anymore. Now she's like... Pissed-off Penny.

"I thought it was an incredibly rigorous task asking students to look at an actual bill and the current policies affecting them. Students should know their rights as students and the educational expectations placed on schools."

"Isn't that nice... Well, admin wants it down."

"So then I need a new lesson for that day?"

"Yes," Penny confirms.

"Which is next week?"

"Again, yes."

"So you, my department chair, are telling me I need to create a new lesson to teach next week, even though the school policy is that *all* lessons must be posted online for two weeks prior for community input?"

I imagine Giselle dropping a microphone and walking out, but in reality, she's still sitting and doesn't appear to be as aggravated as Penny is by this point. It doesn't look like she's trying to have a mic-drop moment. It seems like she's *actually* concerned for her students.

Penny takes a deep breath, and I can see her working hard to keep her calm. "Good point. No, don't create a new lesson. Just move on with the lessons already posted."

"But that lesson taught students to cite textual evidence from a legal document. If I don't teach that lesson, they'll miss out."

"Giselle, you didn't even get the legal document approved as a supplemental text. You don't get to look at laws with students unless the supplemental text has been approved. And the same goes with these policies—the policies are *not* school-approved supplemental texts."

"No, they're widely available public documents that my students all read on their own. I didn't provide them with the laws *or* the policies. I just have a *very* civic-minded group of students this year. What can I say?"

Penny rolls her eyes and stands up. She effectively ends their conversation with, "Giselle, change the lesson."

She walks out before Giselle can respond.

<h1 style="text-align:center">18</h1>

As the first semester comes to a close, I repeat my Friday ritual after school by pulling up my student info spreadsheet and sending Remind messages to several families. I text all the students I haven't seen in a while with encouraging messages. I texted a few of the parents in my first period, hoping they would support my effort to get their students to stop with anti-LGBTQ language. I finish off parent contacts with a reminder to all failing students that I'm available before and after school for tutoring.

Not a single parent responds to my emails or texts. They never do, so I guess I shouldn't be surprised. But it's almost the end of the semester, and it seems like nearly half the students are failing my class—and that's with the district's minimum 50% policy.

If grades reflected actual assignments submitted, most students with between 50 and 60 percent in the class would have between 5 and 10 percent instead. I guess failing is failing, so I shouldn't be so upset. But it seems like parents think their student is significantly closer to passing than they really are. Even if their padded grade is a 57%, the odds that the student will have learned enough to score high enough on a summative assessment to bring that number up to a passing score of 60% seem low.

I feel like giving students an entire class period to catch up on missing assignments at least once a week. It's such a waste of class time, but I don't know how else to get them to do their assignments. And that's just for the kids that show up. It doesn't matter how many study hall days I give my students if they aren't *showing up* to do any of the work.

Since the pandemic, districts have started requiring all materials to be available for student access online. During the pandemic, students proved they *could* be fully functional from home. They could actually access the materials, complete the work, and show up during office hours for help when needed. Apparently, all those skills went out the window the day brick and mortar school buildings opened back up. Daily, students ask me where to find their assignments and what to do— despite the painstakingly detailed instructions I've attempted for each assignment.

We're coming to the end of the semester, and a ton of my students are failing. I'm contacting parents, but I'm getting zero response from them. I'm giving students extra class time, but the kids who already do their work don't need the class time, and those who don't do their work don't use the extra class time either.

It's starting to feel incredibly pointless to put this much effort into my lesson plans and get so little back from students. Why am I staying up until 9 or 10 at night grading papers and creating lessons when students never look at my feedback and only a fraction of the students ever participate in the lessons anyway?

I can feel myself quickly spiraling into a depressed funk, so I decide to change up the scenery. Rather than dwell on the inevitable, I choose to go work on Pride Alliance posters in Giselle's room.

When I finally make my way to Giselle's room, there are already four students working on the posters. I knock lightly on the propped-open door and say, "Hey, am I interrupting?"

The students kneeling on the floor painting posters look up at me, and I see it's Erin, Jax, Sabrina, and a student I haven't met yet.

"Not at all," Giselle calls from the back of the room, her head stuck in a cupboard full of art supplies she's rummaging around in. Giselle is a mess. When she finally stands up, buckets of poster paint in her hands, I can see the paint splotches all over her elbows and the backs of her arms. Her blonde, frizzy hair is pulled into a messy ponytail, only half of her short hair willing to be wrangled by her hair tie. Her smile is wide and genuine, but her eyelids look heavy, and her shoulders are slumped. She looks exhausted.

"Come on in, Sam. You feel like painting?" she asks hopefully.

"Sure…" I say, dragging out the word to subtly convey my lack of artistic ability.

"Great! Grab some butcher paper next to my desk and whatever paint you'd like from around the room. And, if you're feeling extra sparkly, there's tons of glitter in the supply caddies next to Erin."

Erin moves to guard the glitter and gives me a determined look as they say, "Glitter! My precious!"

"I'll pass on the glitter, but thanks," I say, smiling despite my mood. I remember a bunch of YouTube videos and TikTok videos during the pandemic of people using glitter to teach kids how to wash their hands. My mom tried it with my 3-year-old cousin, Remy, when he visited us after the first quarantine. That was three years ago, and I still find glitter in the bathroom. Immediately turning down any use of glitter has now become a gut reaction.

I cut a long piece of butcher paper and ask Giselle, "What should the poster say?"

"Any of the info from the board," she says, pointing. I look at the Promethean board and see *Day of Silence, April 2nd, speak out against discrimination of the LGBTQ+ community by taking a vow of silence for the day, P.R.I.D.E. Alliance sponsored.*

I find a desk with minimal carved-in graffiti, then set my paper down to choose paint colors. As I look through my options, I wonder what the acronym P.R.I.D.E. stands for. "Tell me about the name of your club," I say to Erin, who happens to be still bogarting the glitter.

"People Respecting Individual Differences and Equality," they say.

I like it. It's not specific to the LGBTQ+ community, but the words "pride" and "equality" are often buzzwords when discussing it. Once again, the Shipman High P.R.I.D.E. Alliance students impress me. Although at this point, it doesn't take much; pretty much any student that doesn't swear at me impresses me.

"We've had a hard time getting people to join, though."

"Really?" I'm not honestly shocked by this. I haven't seen many kids openly gender-diverse in their behavior or dress. Conversely, I've seen dozens of kids using anti-LGBTQ language and slurs on campus.

"Well, most people think if you are part of the club, you're gay. And even then, only the bravest kids will come because of that. So, we've got a long way to go on the 'alliance' part of our club name." Erin is disappointed but quickly changes the subject. "Before Ms. Hawkins got here, we didn't even have a club!"

"Really?" I ask. This time, I really *was* shocked. "You started this club?"

"Well, yeah. On my first day as a teacher here at Shipman, a student asked me to speak to me after class at the end of the first period of the first day of school. Once everyone left the room, she told me she was gay, nobody knew, and she wanted to kill herself. That pretty much solidified my resolve for creating the club."

"Holy shit," I mumble. I realize what I've just said and quickly put both hands over my mouth, getting light blue and purple paint specks all over my face.

The four students listening to the conversation laugh, and one of them says, "Oooh, Ms. Hawkins, she has to pay the swear pig!"

All 4 of the kids start chanting, "Swear pig! Swear pig! Swear pig!"

"What's a swear pig?" I ask, covered in embarrassment but feeling more of a sense of belonging than I ever have. Despite my expletive slip-up, my anxiety is nowhere to be seen. The butterflies must be hibernating... or perhaps that's the flutter I feel around my heart and the warmth I feel in my chest right now.

"Meet Nerdy, the swear pig!" Giselle holds up a faded blue plastic piggy bank. The pig wears glasses and a bow tie and has "2011" painted on the side. "Students have to pay 10 cents or give me 10 minutes after school to come up with more school-appropriate alternatives for their swear words. But really, I'll accept any coin. The money goes back to the students when they ask me for bus or lunch money."

I am completely in awe of this woman. We have to be friends. She has a piggy bank named "Nerdy the Swear Pig." She uses the money for students who are in need. She's bizarre but compassionate. I feel like I've finally met someone I can click with...

"So what happened with the student that came out to you?"

"I'm right here," says the fourth student in the room that I hadn't recognized earlier. She's lying on her stomach in front of an impressive pencil sketch of a girl with tape over her mouth.

"Wow, that picture is really good!" I say, hoping to change the subject. I know my anxiety hasn't crept in yet, but I don't think discussing a student while they're in the room is the best plan of action to keep it at bay.

"Thanks," she says, then gets back to her drawing.

"We figured it out, and we created P.R.I.D.E. Alliance. Right, Sophia?" Giselle asks.

"We sure did." Her voice is even-keeled and a stark contrast to Giselle's constant loud enthusiasm. Compared to Giselle, she almost sounds depressed.

"Alright, my peep-a-doodles, we've got ten more minutes before we have to be off-campus for the day, so let's start cleaning up," Giselle instructs. The kids groan but oblige.

I return my paint brushes to their respective buckets and roll up the poster I was working on. "Same time next week?" I ask.

"You bet!" Giselle smiles and waves at me as I leave.

The following week is the last week of school before winter break. That means it's spirit week. Monday's theme is "anything but a backpack." I thought about participating, but twice this month, I've been stopped by our campus monitors to ask what class I'm supposed to be in. Teachers and students must wear their IDs around their necks, so there's no real way to tell us apart, I guess. You know, except by looking at us.

Before my first block of the day, Sabrina stops by with Erin to show me their creativity. Sabrina is practically glowing while she shows me her empty box of fruity pebbles that cleverly contains her Chromebook. Erin proudly models the large stock pot they carry around with their computer and notebooks.

I'm surprised Jax isn't with them, but I remember Jax's mom saying their anxiety would sometimes keep them from going to school. I hope that's not the case here. They wave goodbye and head to their respective classes.

Tuesday's theme is "tourist," and students try their best to dress like tourists. I see a few Hawaiian shirts with khaki shorts, sun hats, and selfie sticks. One student even carries around a translation book of common phrases in German and tries to speak to his seemingly annoyed friends in German only.

Wednesday is "Decades Day," so students attempt to represent the 70's, 80's, and 90's with bright colors and elaborate hairstyles. This is the one day where it looks like more faculty and staff participated than students. Perfectly teased bangs, side ponytails, bell-bottoms, and denim jackets make a comeback.

Thursday's theme is "senior citizens," and I thoroughly enjoy the school spirit on this one. One of my quiet students, Paul, comes to class in flannel pajama pants, a baggie t-shirt with slippers, glasses, and an actual walker. I chuckle as he *slowly* hobbles into the room and finds his seat. For a student that never speaks in class, I'm surprised this is the spirit day he chose to participate in. I'm glad I get a glimpse of his personality.

By Friday, everyone is ready for winter break. Well, everyone except for me. I haven't seen Jax this week, which makes me nervous. A few of Jax's last song selections have been rather dark and depressing, and I really want to check up on them. Today is the last day for my students to finish the last paragraphs of their "Soundtrack of Your Life" assignment. My goal is to grade all of them before I head home after school today. To make that happen, I hustle hard to get the kids to turn them in today.

Once the day is over, I sit down to grade the students' last assignment. I've really enjoyed getting to know them through their assignments, but I've enjoyed seeing their writing improve even more. I think doing the *same* assignment with different content so many times has helped their paragraph writing. I'm looking forward to doing some essays during the second semester.

As I thumb through the stack of papers, it dawns on me that I'll never get the stack graded before I leave today. In addition to this week's assignment, motivated by the end of the semester panic, students have turned in multiple paragraphs. I pull out the shortest ones that look easiest to grade. I figure I can grade the longer, more challenging ones at home with a bottle of wine. I've pulled out papers from Oliver, Sabrina, and Jax. I only have about 20 minutes before I need to head home, so I anticipate getting through these pretty quickly.

Oliver's final song choice is "Break Stuff" by Limp Bizkit. I've never heard the song, but I enjoy his detailed explanation. The singer talks about being angry for no reason, and apparently, Oliver has felt like that a lot throughout his adolescence. He says he joined the soccer team to vent his frustrations, and that song is now his power song when he's trying to get fired up. I make a mental note to check out the song if I ever start exercising.

Sabrina's final song choice is "My Shot" from the musical *Hamilton*. She writes about how the song gives her hope and motivates her. This song reminds her that she must stay focused in school to take her "shot" whenever it comes. I admire her optimism and determination. She keeps turning out to be a cooler kid than I expected.

The final paper I picked up to grade is Jax's.

The last song on the soundtrack for my life would be "Never Let it Die" by Watsky. The song has a lot of great lines, but I'll mention just a few. In one part of the song, Watsky talks about feeling like you've been defeated. When I was 12, my birth mom discovered I wasn't the little girl she had always dreamed of, and she sent me to a "rehabilitation" program for kids that were behavior problems. It was advertised as a boarding school that would cure all your parenting problems. I know some kids were there because they were caught smoking weed, but mostly it was just... kids.

When we arrived at the center, the first thing the leaders did was break us down. They take away any feeling of dignity or self-respect and replace it with shame and humiliation. They convinced me that I was a drug addict and deprived me of sleep, food, and human connection. I wasn't allowed any contact with my parents, though that's the way my parents probably preferred it. After six months of torture, I ran away. A family nearby was known for helping kids escape. That's how I eventually ended up in foster care with my current mom.

When I was at the center, I felt defeated. But like Watsky says later in the song, I kept marching into the darkness and trying to be the light. I didn't let them snuff out my light at the center. I just kept marching. There were times when I didn't think I would survive another day, times where I would plan my death, but here I am.

I drop Jax's assignment on the desk in front of me. My eyes are stinging as I try not to cry.

19

My winter break starts with self-inflicted torture: grading. I somehow convinced myself that getting all the grading done during the first few days of vacation would allow for ultimate relaxation during the rest of it.

I spent that first Saturday morning grading the remaining Soundtrack of Your Life paragraphs. While doing so, I reread Jax's paper three times. I have no idea if this is the type of thing that must be reported. They mentioned it was in the past—in the *past,* they planned their death. And why wouldn't they?

Jax said they grew up feeling they were in the wrong body or being told they were... wrong. Then they ended up at a "rehabilitation camp" that further stripped them of their dignity. All of that led to running away and ending up in foster care. And now, according to the ACLU, transgender youth are experiencing some of the most aggressive attacks in our history.

If you grow up believing you aren't good enough, and you have it further ingrained in you at the rehabilitation camp, then the entire United States of America seems to have a problem with your existence—so much so that they want to ban discussion of your existence in a classroom—why *would* you want to be alive?

But now, Jax has a loving parent who showed up at Back to School to inform teachers of their preferred pronouns. So… perhaps it's not worth reporting?

I deliberate over the matter so much that my head hurts. Finally, I decided to err on the side of caution and fill out the Google form created for this exact purpose. If Jax is suicidal, I don't want to risk their life. After filling out the form, I commit to putting all work out of my mind until winter break is over.

By January, I've learned to budget appropriately for Dutch Bros. coffee once a week. It has become what I most look forward to on Mondays, so I don't mind the occasional splurge. And if it weren't for Dutch Bros. coffee this morning, I might not have gotten out of bed at all.

I remember loving the first Monday back after a long break as a student. I would be excited to work on the upcoming projects in all of my classes, probably because of my social anxiety. I was too awkward to talk to my peers, so I mostly kept my head in my books.

However, this Monday, I am significantly less excited to be back at school. I think I feel *more* exhausted than before the break, only now I have to pick up the pace in my classroom. Penny has planned for her classes to read *Romeo and Juliet,* so I plan to do the same.

We have our next PLC meeting after school today, and I'm optimistic it will end with more supplemental materials than just the meditation videos Diogo submitted. I still can't believe we had virtually zero supplemental materials for the first semester. I'm more shocked that the district is willing to sacrifice learning for parental comfort. At least, that's what it seems like they're doing.

I haven't had any more parental complaints about my

lessons, but that's probably because I've stuck to copying Penny's plans. I figured I couldn't get into trouble if I taught the same thing she was teaching.

My first-period students trickle in slowly throughout the class period. Most look as enthusiastic about being back as I am. By the end of the block period, most students have arrived. I give them the period to review for their first-semester final exams since I don't expect them to remember everything they learned after a three-week vacation. And whose idea was it to have finals *after* winter break?

During my second block period of the day, I realize I haven't seen Jax today. I also realize I never got a response to the Google form I filled out. I don't even know if somebody read it. How do counselors even handle that during winter break? Who is responsible for checking those forms when all the adults are off work?

Later in the day, I get an email from the elusive Ms. Morris—the administrator apparently in charge of doing my evaluations. According to her email, my first two evaluations should have been done by now, and she's scrambling to fit them in. She asked me to pick a day within the next week that I'd like to be observed, so now I'm nervous. I've never met Ms. Morris; I won't even know who she is when she comes to observe me. The scarier thing, though, is that I only get *one week* to prepare whatever I'm going to be evaluated on.

Since none of the lessons are my own creation, I'm not sure it matters which day Ms. Morris chooses to observe. I know I will be absurdly nervous whichever day she comes, so I pick Monday to get it over with as quickly as possible, email her my reply, and get back to teaching.

Once students have finished and the final bell rings for the day, I have about 15 minutes to kill until our next PLC meeting starts. A few students stay behind a minute to draw on the whiteboard before saying goodbye and leaving.

The fourth PLC meeting of the year is held in Giselle's room, which I'm grateful for. Hers is the only classroom I really feel comfortable in. And even though I started the day with my coffee, which I sometimes like to call a hug in a mug, I think I need some support from humans.

I make my way over to Giselle's room and don't bother knocking this time. Her door is held open with a doorstop, so I walk in and sit near the back of the room. Giselle finishes her conversation on the phone before greeting me.

"Hey. How's it going?" she asks casually.

I shrug, my eyes tracing the detailed patterns of the wooden desktop in front of me. I will break down again if I try to answer Giselle's question. There's something about people showing genuine concern that makes me fall apart.

"Do you want to talk about it?" she asks, concerned.

I shake my head and keep looking down. I don't want to start crying before the rest of the teachers get here. Nobody needs to know that I cry over everything. No one needs to see this less-than-professional side of me.

Giselle nods and stands up. She walks over to me, leans down to give me a tight, firm hug, then let's go and walks back to her desk like she hugs me every day. My anxiety is on high alert because of the unexpected hug, but I'm grateful for her kindness.

I start to get a whiff of something musky smelling and look around the room. The scent is shortly joined by the smell of Patchouli—one of my favorite scents in the world. I love woodsy, earthy aromas, so I turn around in my seat to see if there's a diffuser or plug-in somewhere in Giselle's room.

While I'm twisting around like a toddler in a restaurant booth, Diogo strolls casually into the room. His brown, wavy hair is a little puffy today but still looks perfect. Today he's wearing a brown t-shirt with a blue vest over it, blue jeans, and sandals.

His perfect smile, littered with perfect teeth, shines at me, and he says, "Ms. White! What's good?"

I can feel my face heating up in embarrassment. The last thing I need today is to make a fool of myself in front of Diogo. I don't even like him. I don't know a thing about him, but good God, that hair, that skin...

I think about his question but can't find an answer for "what's good" right now. I think about how Jax didn't show up to school today, I haven't gotten a response from the Google form I filled out during the break, and I'm worried they might be a tad suicidal. Add on to that the email regarding my impending evaluation... *I don't know, Diogo. Nothing's good. What's good with you?*

"It's *all* good," I say, trying to sound clever. It's better than the truth, anyway.

"Yes it is, yes it is," he says while selecting a seat. He sits in a purple saucer chair off to the side of the room and crosses his legs in front of him. He folds both hands over his chest, tilts his head back, and closes his eyes. "Wake me when we start," he says.

God, I envy his calm. His zen. I wonder if he really used those meditation videos or just submitted them to be maliciously compliant.

Once Emma and Penny make their way into the classroom, Giselle pelts Diogo with a few Starbursts to wake him up.

"Heeeey," he groans, his eyes still closed. But he feels around his chair blindly for one of the pieces of candy, unwraps it, and pops it in his mouth with a toothy smile. "Thanks."

Penny begins the meeting with her usual reminders about the copy machines breaking down, lack of paper for final exams, and late work policies.

"As students are starting to realize they might fail your classes and ask about late work and extra credit, please keep in mind that Shipman High doesn't allow teachers to penalize students academically for late work. So, you cannot give them less than the amount of credit they actually earned on the assignment."

"Well, they get a 60% for turning the assignment in. How much can we really penalize them anyway?" Giselle points out.

Emma adds, "I think it's pretty safe to say as a PLC, we don't dock students' points for late work."

Although I've never taken points off a late assignment, I can't help but wonder if the other teachers have as many students fails as I do.

Final exams are this Thursday and Friday, and I've told students I would pass them for the entire semester if they passed the final exam. For my final, I curated a multiple-choice test with various questions from CommonLit.org. I'm confident it's a good exam, but I'm not confident in my students' ability to pass it.

I've spent so much time preparing lessons and trying to engage students in the classroom, but so many of them are so apathetic. I'm constantly competing with sleep schedules, hormones, electronics, and real-life issues for their attention. And those are just the students who are actually showing up to class. In either situation, students aren't doing their work or getting a 60% for turning in something with their name on it. As a result, their grade reflects a 60% passing D, albeit barely passing, but passing nonetheless.

So when the students are given an exam with all the skills they should have at least *met* if they're earning a D in the class, they cannot achieve that same 60%. They never reached a 60% in the skill outside the test, so how can they demonstrate a 60% on the test?

My mind is a swirling contradictory mess. I can't make heads or tails of the grading policies and don't remember them being this confusing in college or high school. Luckily, my attention is pulled back to the present when Giselle pelts Diogo with another Starburst, and he protests, "My eyes were open!"

"Great, let's get these kids through the last week of the

semester. We need to get as many of them to pass as we can. We have another full week of mid-year diagnostic tests before the testing window closes. Your students need to have finished testing by the end of this month. We'll look at data and pick our focus standards for the second semester."

"Diogo, you may now sleep," Penny concludes.

Everyone gathers their belongings, and I quietly approach Penny.

"Penny, can I ask you a quick question?"

"Sure!" I'm unsure if her cheeriness is from the three-week winter break we had or that nobody goaded her during the PLC meeting today.

"During vacation, I filled out a Google form for a student I was concerned about. Do you know what the next step is or when the counselors will get to it?"

"Oh," she casually waves her hand, "they probably already did. Once you fill out the form, you're no longer responsible."

"Is there any way for teachers to see counselor notes or get some sort of… reassurance that the concern was actually addressed?" This conversation is more and more concerning.

"Nope. Can you imagine? There are so many students and so few counselors—they'd probably spend most of their day just responding to forms and emails."

Isn't that what they're supposed to be doing? I wonder to myself.

"Alright, well, is there a way I can find out if the counselors spoke to a particular student?"

"Sure, just email them directly. Again, they're not great with responding to emails, so they might not get to it for a while."

"Oh… thanks…" I grab my teaching bag and head back to my classroom. I can't help but wonder about the repercussions of having a system for reporting students who need extra mental health support with so few checks and balances. And I'm not even supposed to talk to the students about their mental health. So, when I see Jax, I'm not supposed to ask if they've seen their counselor or tell them I'm concerned.

The contradictions woven throughout all the different school policies is completely mind-boggling to me. Worst of all, it seems like the people most likely to suffer in this system is the students. If there aren't enough counselors for the number of students we have, then it seems illogical to remove conversations about mental health from the teachers who see them daily and know them by name.

I'm frustrated, and there's nothing I can do about it.

20

By the end of our first week back, students have taken their semester exams, and I'm up to my ears in grading again. I spend the afternoon of the last Friday of the semester grading exams, reluctant to take any work home with me.

"Hey, Miss?" I hear a voice from the propped-open door and look up from my grading.

"Jax! How's it going?" I ask cheerfully. I haven't seen Jax since the week before winter break, and I couldn't possibly be happier. I've been worried about them all winter break and every day this week. I even emailed a couple of their teachers to check if they'd been to class this week.

"I was wondering if I could talk to you about some personal stuff."

"Of course!" My stomach knots up in anticipation of whatever Jax needs to talk about. Are students allowed to talk to us about personal stuff? Does that cross the line into mental health? What exactly counts as mental health?

On top of that, I feel overly-protective and extra cautious about Jax. I want to protect them from anything else horrible happening in their life. I want to protect them from the cruel comments from their peers and society's expectations of how they should look and identify. I want to protect them from horrible rehabilitation centers that strip them of their dignity. I want to protect them from "that's gay" and parents that don't understand them.

But I'm not allowed to talk to them about any of that.

I move to a desk near the side of the room and gesture for Jax to join me. Their ripped jeans are paired with a white hoodie and their trademark beat-up white Chucks. They sit at the desk next to me and drop their backpack on the floor.

"So, what's up?" I ask, feeling the familiar butterflies in my stomach starting to flutter. My breathing is getting shallower, too, but I try to focus on Jax. I know I can't ask about whether or not any counselors got in touch with them, but I'm hoping they might divulge that information anyway.

"Okay, so you know how my deadname is Brianna?" I know Jax is referring to their legal name. Last week, they complained about a teacher using their "deadname" in class, so even if Jax's mom hadn't informed me before school started, I know Brianna is not a name we use.

"Okay, and you know how my pronouns are 'they' and 'them'?" Jax's voice sounds confident, which is nice since I'm confused about where this is heading.

"Yes..." My voice trails off, and an eyebrow raises expectantly.

"Okay, well, I don't use they or them pronouns anymore."

"Okay..."

"My pronouns are now 'he' and 'him,'" Jax asserts.

My eyebrows shoot up, and I say, "Okay. Do I still call you Jax?"

"Yeah, I'm still going by Jax for now. But you can use 'he' and 'him' pronouns."

The importance of this moment is not lost on me. I can't imagine how difficult it would be to tell someone I'd prefer different pronouns than the ones I currently use—whether they were assigned to me at birth or not. But... I don't think I can relay that to Jax. Would it be crossing a line?

"Thank you for telling me, Jax. It means a lot that you felt comfortable enough to share that with me," I say, resting my hand on Jax's desk across from me.

"Yeah… do you think you could tell the rest of the class for me? Just to make things easier?" he asks.

Oh, boy.

I'm going to announce Jax's preferred pronouns after learning the board member's daughter, my department chair's niece, is also in my class. They are in different periods, thankfully, but word gets around. I haven't heard other teachers publicly addressing a student's gender preference in front of the class.

"Of course, I can do that," I say with feigned confidence. "How about I do it at the start of our next class together?"

Jax nods and seems to zone out for a minute while I'm deep in thought about how I will announce this to the class. And whether or not it's going to be the end of my career at Shipman High.

"I'm gonna be out of town for the first two weeks of February," he says.

"Oh! Okay. Where are you going?"

Jax is rarely here, so a two-week vacation at the start of the second semester seems ill-advised to me. But it's not my place to say so. My place is to sit here, comforting Jax as vaguely as possible.

"I have a doctor in San Francisco that I've been seeing since I was 13, so I'm going to see them."

"That must be an *amazing* doctor to warrant that kind of drive for an appointment."

"Well, yeah, Miss. Doctors refuse to treat transgender kids in our state."

Transgender. Jax is transgender.

The label hadn't occurred to me before.

Jax just admitted to being transgender.

We have a policy requiring we report transgender kids. I

don't even know who we report it to or what happens—just that we're supposed to report it. Am I going to have to report what Jax is telling me? I'm dizzy with worry, and it's getting harder and harder to keep my breathing slow and even.

"Doctors here don't treat transgender kids?" The question pops out of my mouth before I can stop it, and my hands immediately cover my mouth in disbelief.

"I mean, they do, but only as the sex they were assigned at birth. I'm not a girl, so I need to see a doctor that understands that."

Wow. I can't imagine having to hop the state line just to get healthcare. I can't imagine what I would do if the government suddenly decided anyone with my pronouns or gender identity didn't get health care anymore. How does that even work?

"So you've had this doctor for a while?"

"Yeah, since I ran away from the boarding school."

The boarding school. He must be talking about the rehabilitation center his mom sent him to. I'm dying to ask him about it, but I don't want to pry. Actually, I really, really want to pry, but I won't because I've already had to report Jax's potential for self-harm; I'm actively discussing a forbidden topic with a student, *and* that student has just confirmed they are transgender.

I might have to report that Jax is transgender to someone.

"Okay, so your doctor is in another state. You'll be back within two weeks. Are you vacationing while you're there, too?" I ask, trying to make small talk. Perhaps if we change the subject, I can forget he's transgender... or forget that I'm supposed to report it.

"Not really. We might do some touristy stuff, but it's just so I can start my new meds and see how they affect me. Since it's so expensive and takes so much time to get there, we try to get as much taken care of in one trip as possible."

"Oh, are you okay? Is your health okay?" I ask, concerned. As soon as I hear the phrase "new meds," I assume mental health issues, so I'm hyper-vigilant again. And in my hyper-vigilance, I realize that I keep asking questions I'm not supposed to. We've been talking for a few minutes now, and my breathing has slowed to normal.

"Yeah, I'm going to start hormone therapy," he says.

"Oh!" I exclaim. "Okay, gotcha. So in about two weeks, you'll know how it's affecting you and head back to school?"

At this point, I want just to end this conversation as quickly as possible. The more time we talk, the more information I'm responsible for.

"Yeah. Can you email me my assignments?"

"I will definitely keep everything posted on Google Classroom," I confirm.

"Okay, thanks, Miss. I gotta get home, but I wanted to talk to you about the pronouns for class tomorrow."

"Yes, I will make sure to inform the class," I say determinedly, although I had forgotten entirely once Jax started talking about his doctor appointment.

"Bye, Miss." Jax gets up, slings his backpack over his shoulder, and leaves.

Once Jax is gone, I let my head fall onto the desk, resulting in a dull pain and a loud thud.

I know I probably have plenty of nonbinary and transgender students; they just don't talk about it. On the other hand, Jax has spent the entire year figuring out who they are and proudly asked to inform his peers. He's ready to be himself in front of his peers—something some teenagers are *never* prepared for. And instead of celebrating with Jax, I'm worrying and deliberating.

I wonder if the students were ever informed about the new policies. Did anyone tell them they're not allowed to talk about gender and sexuality at school? Did anyone tell them that transgender kids were being reported? That transgender kids are just... *kids?*

I lift my head and stand up from the student desk I've folded myself into. My body feels heavy. My shoulders are sagging in a way I can't fix by standing up straighter. My heart is heavy in a way I can't fix with a hug and some ice cream.

What *is* the protocol for reporting transgender students? And why do we have to report them anyway?

I somehow make my way over to my teacher's desk, sit on my crappy, broken chair, and search Google Drive for a form for reporting transgender students. I'm hoping I can find some explanation while I'm searching to make me feel better about possibly reporting Jax. Right now, the fact that Jax didn't mention the counselor checking up on him gives me hope that the Google forms are altogether unnecessary. If no one reads them anyway, what's the point of filling them out?

And what happens if I *don't* report Jax? Would anyone ever know? Would anyone ever care?

I find a shared folder with various Google forms, but other than a title and request for identifying information, the forms offer nothing in the way of potential consequences. I think I should talk to someone before filling out more forms. Or before I decide *not* to.

With the decision made, I click out of the browser and walk to Giselle's room.

While walking to Giselle's classroom, I feel my eyes begin to sting and the familiar tickle of impending tears. I try to walk quicker, but before I know it, silent tears have spilled over, and they keep coming. When I get to Giselle's room, I knock before pulling the door open and poking my head in.

I see Giselle sitting at her desk grading, and I choke out, "Are you busy?"

She finally looks up from the paper she's been reading and makes eye contact with me. As soon as she sees my face, she immediately replaces her look of boredom with one of deep concern.

"Hey, yeah, come on in, Sam," she says. Her voice is comforting, like hot chocolate on a cold day. It's so reassuring that my silent stream of tears turns into full-on bawling while I stand in her doorway.

Giselle walks over and takes my arm. She leads me to the fuzzy purple saucer chairs in the corner of her room and motions for me to sit. She grabs a box of tissues and hands them to me before sitting beside me and placing a hand on my upper back.

"Hey, it's okay. What's going on?" Her voice is worried and comforting at the same time. It's the voice my mom used when Stacy died. It's the voice my mom uses whenever she sees me cry. It's a mother's voice, and somehow that voice is exactly what sent me into this ugly-crying fit.

Once I've gotten enough heaving sobs out of my system, I manage to answer Giselle's question. "I'm really overwhelmed, and I don't know how to do this. How are we supposed to care about our students without caring about our students? How are we supposed to tell students they can't share any personal information with us?" My voice is squeaky, my face feels like a puffy mess, and I keep picturing the scene with my family at Denny's—the one where they told me I wouldn't survive as a teacher.

"I have a transgender student, and I don't know what I'm supposed to do. What happens if I don't report it?"

Giselle's lips turn up slightly on one side, and she says with an empathetic voice, "I don't know." She rubs my back reassuringly, and I start bawling again. She just sits there and lets me cry. She doesn't ask me a million questions; she doesn't show any judgment about the implication that I might not report it. She just sits next to me, rubbing my back.

"Why do they want us to report it? Is the student in trouble?" The concern in my voice is audible even to me.

"You know what, I don't know," she says. "Let me text Penny really quickly and see if she has any insight. She ought to since she wrote the damn policies." Giselle walks back to her desk to grab her cell phone and proceeds to text Penny. She returns to sit next to me with her phone.

I'm silent now, but tears are still streaming down my face. I have never felt less professional, even when jumping on the cockroach dictionary at the beginning of the year.

"Do you want to tell me what happened?" she asks gently. Her voice has no sense of expectation, and it's refreshing.

"I have a student that came to talk to me after school today—just a few minutes ago. They told me their pronouns are now 'he' and 'him'. They want *me* to inform the class, and they're going to be out of town for a few weeks for some doctor's appointments."

Giselle nods with understanding, then looks down at the vibrating phone in her hands.

"Oh! Penny texted back. She said the reports are used to investigate child abuse. So when you fill out the form, they send it to the social workers on campus to ensure the student is safe at home. She says that's how all the Google Forms work."

Intense relief floods my system, and I ask, "So Jax can't get into trouble for being transgender?"

"Well, I mean... regardless of what steps the school takes, he's a person and deserves to be treated with dignity and respect. They can't tell kids they can't *be* transgender; they just don't want to deal with the ramifications of having transgender students. Then they'd have to do things like ameliorate the dress code and provide single-stall bathrooms for students."

I guess Giselle has a point. They can't punish Jax for being transgender. What are they going to do, suspend him?

I think about the abuse investigation Giselle mentioned. I wonder if that would be so bad. I don't know a ton about Jax, but I know his birth mom didn't appreciate that he didn't identify as female; I know she sent him to a boarding school where he says he was abused, and I know he ran away and somehow ended up in his current living situation. What if investigating the abuse could get Jax some closure or mental health support?

Then I think about whether or not Jax would want any of that. Shouldn't he get some say in whether or not his whole childhood is brought to light? This whole thing is ridiculous. I'm 21 years old; I shouldn't be trying to decide the fate of a 15-year-old. I barely have more life experience than he does!

"Okay, so what happens if I don't report it?" I ask again. "I mean… I'm announcing it to the class for him when I update the students on his pronouns…"

"Well, more than likely, no one will ever know. I don't know if another teacher could report the student and if you could get in trouble for knowing and not reporting it. Still, if reporting it could potentially stop some abuse that's happening at home, then you've got a really tough decision on your hands."

Ugh. She's right. It would be easy to pretend I don't know what I know. What would it matter to anyone if I didn't report it? Then again, if Jax *is* being abused at home and I don't report it, it could mean the world. It could mean safety. But Jax's birth mom didn't allow him to be himself, and it seems like his current mom is supportive.

What do I do?

21

The next morning, I'm nervous about updating the class on Jax's pronouns. I'm not quite sure how to go about it, but I'm also worried that I will get reprimanded again for it as soon as Penny hears that I addressed the entire class to discuss pronoun changes. Who knows what the fallout will be?

I'm also worried about how this will affect Jax. I'm the only one who knows his pronouns have changed. If I don't report Jax being transgender, another student or faculty member could. I could get into trouble for having the knowledge and *not* reporting it. And what if it turned out Jax *was* being abused at home? Would I ever be able to forgive myself?

But what if I report it, and Jax feels betrayed? How do you explain to a kid, "I have to report that you're transgender…" Is the expectation that we are secret police and *don't* tell the students? God, I feel like I'm in a contemporary version of *1984.*

I stand outside my classroom door with a cup of Dutch Bros. coffee. Coffee is my hug in a mug. I feel like I deserved a hug before I deal publicly with pronouns. I smile and fist-bump students as they walk in, but my brain is entirely focused on the announcement I'll make to the class in three minutes. If I'm this nervous, I wonder how Jax is feeling.

This whole time, I haven't even stopped to consider what it must be like for Jax to have to tell all their peers that they use a different pronoun. The questions he might get, the comments, the looks, the whispers... And if I don't announce it to the class, he's left to correct everyone when they refer to him for the rest of the year. He's taking a significant risk. If he's brave enough to take this risk, why shouldn't I be?

Sabrina walks Jax to class this morning and stops just outside the door.

"Okay, I made Jax come to class today. He was totally gonna ditch."

Jax looks at Sabrina, pretend shock covering his pierced face. Today, Jax is wearing eyeliner, lipstick, and a black skirt that looks more like a kilt. Today, I will tell Jax's peers that the person wearing makeup and a skirt uses 'he' and 'him' pronouns. Even though he's wearing makeup. And a skirt. God, I can imagine the things that might come from students' mouths... How am I going to protect Jax from any adverse consequences from this?

"Well, I'm so glad," I say honestly. "Jax, are we still making that announcement to the class today?"

"Yes, definitely," he says, nodding. I notice he has some new piercings. One on the inside of his upper lip. It's pierced on the inside and looks like a horseshoe. He has a second one on his bottom lip—also a horseshoe shape, but facing up.

My thoughts go through zero filtering process, and I ask, "Okay, how many times have your mouth piercings gotten stuck together?"

My face goes slightly red once I realize what I've just asked. It's not like me to say something without it going through my anxiety filter. You know, it's like a strainer or sieve. The things that might cause embarrassment or panic attacks stay behind, and only the "safe" comments pass through.

"Zero! That hasn't happened. But this one always gets stuck on my top teeth," he said, pointing to the piercing behind his upper lip. He then twists the piercing to show how it gets caught in his teeth.

"Miss, it's okay. It doesn't hurt," he says, laughing. I realize my face has contorted into a remarkably uncomfortable-looking expression. And I *am* incredibly uncomfortable.

"Wow! Soooo gross!" I say, then sip my coffee in an attempt to fix my expression. If I keep thinking about Jax's piercing getting stuck on his teeth, I might tear my hair out. It feels how nails on a chalkboard *sound*.

"Okay, get to class, Jax. I'll see you after," Sabrina says. She stands on her tiptoes and kisses Jax on the cheek. He blushes and says, "Yes, ma'am."

Jax enters the classroom and finds his seat. Once the final bell rings, I join the students in the room.

"Good morning, lovely students!" I say enthusiastically. I plan to be assertive and leave no room for questions. Because I can't answer any questions. And I am so, so worried about the consequences of what I'm about to do.

"While working on your warm-ups, your classmate wanted me to make an announcement." None of the students are looking at me. They're all staring mindlessly at their cell phones or rummaging through their bags for their notebooks and Chromebooks—typical first-period behavior.

"So… Jax wanted to let everyone know that he uses 'he' and 'him' pronouns. So, if you're talking about Jax, it's 'he' or 'him' pronouns." I say it quickly and matter-of-factly.

A few students stop rummaging through their bags, and Cody says, "Wait—who?"

"Jax," I say, pointing. I watch Cody turn to look at Jax behind him. He noticeably drops his eyes to Jax's skirt. Then back to his face. Then back to his skirt before turning around.

"Okay." Cody goes back to rummaging through his

belongings, and the butterflies in my stomach retreat.

No one says anything else about it.

Why do adults always make things seem like they're a bigger deal than they really are?

At lunch, I'm eager to check in with Giselle. I want to tell her about the announcement and get her take on all of it. I don't even bother heating my Hot Pocket today. Instead, I walk quickly toward Giselle's room.

Before I make it to her room, though, I see Mr. Sanders talking to Penny. When he notices me headed in his direction, he seems to say goodbye, and Penny walks away without glancing in my direction.

When I approach, he moves to stand next to me and awkwardly puts his arm around my shoulder. This is the first time any boss of mine has ever touched me, and my social anxiety doesn't like it. My body is on high alert, and I can feel the "fight or flight mode" kicking into overdrive.

"Ms. White," he says, dragging out my last name. "You have the highest number of F's of anyone on campus."

The blood from my face drains, and things are getting a bit fuzzy. Whenever I have an actual panic attack, I feel like I'm dying and have zero control over my body. My method for managing my panic attacks has mostly been focused on preventing them from happening.

I couldn't have prevented this.

"I do?" I ask in disbelief.

"You do. You have more than any other teacher. That can't happen again."

What does he mean it can't happen again? What am I supposed to do to get kids to pass? Students don't show up to school and don't get reprimanded by the district aside from an attendance letter sent to an address that might not even be accurate. Within the last few years, the district adopted an entirely new grading policy in which every student gets a 50%

for every assignment—even if they don't do the assignment. They don't even have to attempt it. They just get an automatic 50%. This means that if they even write their name on a piece of paper, they get an automatic 60%. If students won't even put their name on a piece of paper for the 60%, what options do I really have as the teacher?

"Oh… okay…" My voice sounds far away to me, but it could have to do with the imminent panic attack. I'm lightheaded and dizzy and can't manage to keep my breathing steady. I know my face is as red as can be, and it's taking every ounce of effort in my body to stave off the impending tears. All I can think about is getting away from Mr. Sanders before I start crying.

"You need to offer a recovery assignment. It can be anything you want, but you need to try to get as many of those kids to pass as you can. At least 30% of the fails."

I'm utterly dumbfounded. I've emailed missing assignments to families every week this year. I've texted and emailed home weekly for student concerns and praises. And I've bugged kids daily during class to be on task. I've done everything short of completing their assignments *for* them. What else am I supposed to do?

"Oh…" I say, still dumbfounded.

"You have until February 1st to get me those grade changes."

"Oh…" I'm sure my verbal skills are causing Mr. Sanders to wonder if the money he allocated for my wages could have been put to better use.

"See you later, Ms. White."

With that, he squeezes my shoulder before removing his arm, adjusting his sunglasses, and walking away.

I keep my head down and walk back to my classroom as quickly as possible, desperate to get behind a closed door before I begin crying. Again.

I sit at the first student desk by the door, crying into my hands. I feel so ridiculous. Why did I ever think I could do this? Why did I believe skipping student teaching was a good idea? Why did I think my family was wrong when they told me I shouldn't become a teacher?

I let myself sob for several minutes. My ego is bruised, but I'm a first-year teacher. I shouldn't even have an ego. I should be prepared to make tons of mistakes and get things wrong. But I'm not. And I never have been. Mistakes and wrong answers have always made me feel inadequate.

I can't believe I have more students failing than anyone else on campus. How are other teachers getting the kids who aren't showing up to the school to pass their classes? And what did Mr. Sanders mean when he said that it can't happen again?

As if I did this on purpose. As if it were a choice.

When the tears finally stop, and my body feels adequately exhausted, I peel myself out of the desk I'm in and walk to my teacher's desk to use some tissues and fix my makeup. I have about 10 minutes left of lunch before students return to class, and I'm sure it will take me at least that long to pull myself together.

I can't get Mr. Sander's comment from my head: *"It can't happen again."* If I have too many F's, will I be out of a job? In my interview for this job, I remember being asked what I would do if everyone in my class were failing. My answer was that I would reflect on my teaching and what needed to be modified to meet my student's needs. But honestly, now that I'm in it… I don't know what the hell to do.

I'm scared I'm going to lose my job. I'm afraid I won't be rehired next year with all my fails and the way I seem to keep getting myself into predicaments regarding information about students.

Ugh. Jax. I have to decide what to do about Jax.

Mr. Sanders says I have the most fails of anyone on campus, he's already called me in for a meeting about my lessons once this year, and now I have to decide what to do with the information Jax gave me.

I'm too afraid to toe any lines in my first year teaching, and I figure announcing Jax's change in pronouns to the class will inevitably get around school. The best thing to do seems to be reporting Jax… at least, it seems like the best thing to do to help keep my job.

When I get home, I pour myself a large glass of cold Riesling. I quickly down the first glass and pour myself another. I know I will need a lot of liquid courage for this next task.

I take my glass of wine over to the cozy chair by my bed. My over-sized chair always reminds me of a hug. If a piece of furniture could give a hug, this chair totally would. The big arms and extra fluffy pillows I've piled on top of it make it even cozier.

When sufficiently cozy, I use my phone to pull up the Google Form I need to fill out about Jax. It asks for three pieces of information: student name, grade, and ID#. It doesn't have a space for comments or questions, but it does record my email address. I imagine someone will contact me if they have questions.

Once I've submitted the form, I finish my second glass of Riesling and turn *Ted Lasso* on the television. No one makes me feel more optimistic about life than Ted Lasso. I watch in my comfy chair until the Riesling and emotional drain of the day cause me to fall asleep.

22

I don't see Jax in class on Friday and decided to use the weekend to put the whole situation out of my head and focus on the lesson for my evaluation in the upcoming week. I wish I were less nervous about it. When I first scheduled it, I wasn't worried at all. But now that Mr. Sanders has pointed out my fail rate, it seems more important than ever to shine in my evaluation. I'm glad I wasn't bold enough to put my desks into rows.

I found a website for Quality Teaching for English Learners (QTEL) and joined another Facebook teacher group. This group is filled with teachers sharing strategies and lesson ideas using the advertised QTEL strategies. I pick one of the strategies to introduce Romeo and Juliet for my evaluation lesson. Although my 'lesson' has been posted online for weeks, I knew I needed to improve it before my evaluation.

I'm excited about the new QTEL strategy I find. During the lesson, students will sit in groups of 4. They will take turns listing anything they know about the play or Shakespeare within their groups. One person shares something they know, another person in the group repeats it out loud, then all members write the item down on their list. The goal is for students to have the same list by the end of the activity without looking at each other's papers.

Once lists are complete, every student stands at their desk. One by one, students read an item from their list. Once they've spoken, they sit. Everyone else standing checks their list to either check off the item they already had or add the new item to their list. By the end of the class, every single student had spoken, listened, read, and written. And on top of all that, every student in the room now has roughly the same background knowledge of the play and its playwright.

By Sunday night, I feel confident about my lesson, especially since I'll get to practice it Monday before being evaluated on Tuesday. Hopefully, I can iron out all the kinks and modify the lesson sufficiently before I'm evaluated. Thank God for block schedules.

Monday morning is an even day, which means I don't have any of my odd-period classes. The first period of the day is my prep period, and I use it to reread the first two Acts of Romeo and Juliet. Now that I understand the numerous crude jokes and double entendres, I find I'm no longer quite as impressed by the tragic love story.

During my next period, I get the opportunity to teach the lesson for my evaluation for the first time. It's a small class of about 15 students, and getting them to participate can be pretty tricky. Sometimes, smaller class sizes can make students feel more on display when they participate or make mistakes. At least, that was my experience as a student.

Today, however, every student seems to be participating. I circulate the room and encourage students to follow the structured sentence frames to promote conversation equity. I'm practically giddy as I notice every single student participating and engaged. I'm so proud of them and feel great about the lesson I'm doing for my evaluation.

Class is interrupted before students can complete the activity. A tall, thin, Hispanic woman knocks on my unlocked classroom door, then motions through the tiny window for me to come outside. I tell the students to try to Google something that hasn't already been shared about Shakespeare himself and step out.

The woman wears a gray plaid pencil skirt and a white blouse. Around her neck is a black lanyard with an employee badge and the name *Angela Morris*. I infer that she must be the one observing me, but I'm not supposed to be observed and evaluated until tomorrow. Unless I got the date wrong...

My face flushes red in embarrassment, and I realize that's what must have happened. I must have mixed up the days for my observation, and now I'm off to a *stellar* start in my evaluation process.

Ms. Morris' face is somber, and her thick-framed black glasses magnify her sympathetic brown eyes. She doesn't say anything, and my heart is racing too fast to say anything myself. How could I mess up this badly before finishing my first full year of teaching? Ms. Morris must be feeling pity for the non-reelection notice she's probably ready to hand me, effectively ending my teaching career before it truly began.

Eventually, Ms. Morris's gaze breaks from mine, staring down at her shiny black high-heel shoes. Behind Ms. Morris, Mr. Sanders starts to walk up with Penny, his arm around her shoulders.

"Ms. White, Penny is going to watch your class for a little bit so that Ms. Morris and I can chat with you," Mr. Sander's sympathetic voice says. I can't believe they're going to fire me in the middle of the day. I wonder if I'll get to at least finish off the year teaching or if they will make me leave immediately. I feel a hand clench around my heart as I think about leaving without saying goodbye to Jax and the rest of my students.

"Okay..." My voice sounds thin and uncertain. Penny smiles at me reassuringly and squeezes my shoulder as she enters my classroom. Ms. Morris puts her arm around my shoulder, and I'm starting to doubt this is about a non-reelection notice.

Ms. Morris guides me wordlessly to the principal's conference room, Mr. Sanders trailing behind us. Five other teachers I don't know are sitting around the table when we arrive. Ms. Morris points me to an empty chair and tells me to sit. Confused and trying to stave off complete panic, I sit. The two administrators walk to the head of the room and awkwardly clear their throats a few times, exchanging silent glances that tell us all something terrible is about to be announced.

I look at my colleague's faces, and everyone seems equally uneasy. Teachers shift in their seats and exchange confused glances while waiting for the meeting to begin.

Mr. Sanders finally says, "We called you all in here today because we wanted to give you some privacy when you first heard the news we're about to tell you."

Our eyes quickly meet each other's, scanning one another's faces for clues that don't exist.

"When we tell you this, we need you to keep it private until we announce it to the entire school," Ms. Morris's steady voice adds.

"We got word this morning that a Shipman High student died this weekend."

A collective gasp erupts from the room, and I think back to Penny's shoulder squeeze as she entered my classroom in the middle of the period, and I think about Mr. Sanders' arm around Penny's shoulders when they arrived. It's all starting to fall in place.

I take a slow, deep breath in.

"The student's name was Brianna Stewart."

I exhale even more slowly.

My heart is pounding in my ears. I start to count my heartbeats.

One.

Two.

Three.

Four…

Who's Brianna Stewart?

The rest of the teachers in the room also wrinkle their foreheads in confusion. We all look at each other again, scanning each other's faces for any hint of recognition or reminder of who this was.

And then it clicks.

Jax.

Brianna Stewart is Jax Stewart.

There is no Brianna Stewart. There is a Jax Stewart.

There… was… a Jax Stewart.

"Jax?" I ask skeptically. I hope I'm wrong, but I can't think of another student with the last name Stewart.

Ms. Morris nods her head solemnly.

Recognition is evident on everyone's faces now as they process the news.

"What happened?" I ask, unable to hide my shock.

"She killed herself," Ms. Morris says quietly.

"He." I say it loudly and clearly—one word. I make sure to over-enunciate the letter 'h' as I repeat, "He. *He* killed *him*self."

Ms. Morris gives me a look of pity like this detail was utterly trivial, but I just can't tell in my grief-stricken state.

"Does anyone know why?" A teacher across the table asks.

Ms. Morris and Mr. Sanders look at each other once more before looking back at the teacher who'd asked the question. They both shake their heads, eyes downcast.

"I know this is impossible news. You may finish the day or, if this is too much for you, you have my permission to go home for the rest of the day. We're gathering the counselors to prepare for trauma counseling and announcing it to the rest of the students and staff during announcements tomorrow," Mr. Sanders finishes.

Three of the teachers in the room are sobbing lightly. Ms. Morris' face is slightly puffy and red as though she were recently crying, but Mr. Sanders and I seem to be the only completely dry-eyed people in the room.

My heart has stopped racing, or at least I'm no longer aware of it. Maybe it's because everything feels like it's moving in slow motion. I stand and shakily say, "I'd like to go home, please."

"Absolutely, Amy will get a sub to cover for you the rest of the day. Let us know if you need anything at all, Ms. White." Ms. Morris' voice is kind and comforting. I nod, keep my eyes on the floor, and walk quickly back to my classroom.

I keep my eyes focused on the tiled floor beneath my feet, careful not to step on any cracks—like I used to do when I was a little girl following my parents around in the grocery store. The world was my playground, and I delighted in imagining the lava that seeped from the cracks between the tiles. I'm 21 and relying heavily on the imaginary lava to distract me from reality. If I don't think about it, I might be able to hold off crying until I get to my car.

I imagine the deep red lava of the original Super Mario Brothers games bubbling slightly, each tile square a coin box from the game. Each time I step on a square, I win a coin, like in the game. I count the coins I would earn and by coin 79, I'm back to my classroom.

I keep my head down as I pull open my classroom door quickly. I carefully avoid eye contact with any of my students or Penny as I make a beeline for my desk. I grab my purse from the locked bottom drawer and quickly make my way to the door to leave.

"Miss, can I talk to you? It's really important." Addison, a quiet student who rarely speaks, gestures to me near as I try to leave. I pause for a moment and consider pretending that I didn't hear her. She is one of those students that does every assignment but rarely speaks. I decide that it's worth it to get to hear from her and walk over to her seat near the door, clutching my purse like a security blanket.

I'm careful not to make eye contact with the other students as I kneel next to Addison's desk to privately say, "What's up?"

"Hi, Miss. I just wanted to ask if you're okay…"

My chest tightens, and my eyes sting. I can no longer hold back the tears that start streaming down my face. I give Addison a tight smile and say, "I'm okay. Thank you." I touch her arm briefly and rush out of the room.

When I finally get inside my truck, I lean back against the headrest and close my eyes. I let the tears stream silently down my face for several moments until my face feels puffy and the well seems to have dried up. I start the engine and drive home slowly, feeling like I'm in a trance.

The radio is off, and it's perfect. I don't want to hear any music. Instead, I focus on the speedometer as I drive, glancing down every few seconds. I focus on staying at the exact speed limit, counting to three before I resume driving after stopping at a stop sign, and ensuring that I know what might be in my blind spots. The only sounds are the engine revving after a stop or the clicking of my blinker.

I am in another world.

I finally make it home and inside my bedroom. I walk straight to my closet and dig around in some boxes in the corner of the dark closet until I find what I'm looking for. The dingy Malcom Mushroom Squishmallow my mother bought me the day she told me about Stacy is still just as soft after all these years. I get under the covers, snuggle my Squishmallow and scour the web for anything I can find about Jax or his death.

At some point, someone will probably start a fundraiser. Someone will post something in remembrance of him, or someone will tag the school in a mention of him… I search and search in case there's a way I can see his face again. After several moments of fruitless scrolling, I let my phone fall out of my hand onto the bed, and I cried until I fell asleep.

<h1 style="text-align:center">23</h1>

In my post-sobbing state, I dream of absolutely nothing. I feel like I'm awake but standing in a pitch-black room with no windows and no light. I'm acutely aware that I'm lying in bed until a loud pounding startles me awake.

"Sam, sweetie," I hear my mom call through the closed door. "Dinner is ready!"

I glance at my phone next to me and see that it's already 7:00 P.M. I slept for almost 8 hours. How is that possible?

I sit up and realize I'm still holding my Squishmallow Mushroom, Malcom. I bring the faded polka-dot mushroom cap to my nose and inhale the memories and mental comfort, exhaling my heartache and sadness.

I pull up Jax's contact information from his student profile and write down his Guardian's name, Deb Larson, her number, and address. Before I do anything else, I order flowers to be delivered to Deb with my deepest sympathies on the accompanying card.

I drop my phone back onto my bed and stare at my fingers. Long, thin, pale white fingers with freckles sprinkled liberally about. My pink and green ombre nail polish betrays my actual age of 21. My hands look like I'm 12. I feel like about 60.

I focus on my 4-7-8 breathing, carefully inhaling, holding, and exhaling on the count. I notice my head feeling a bit light and wonder if I'm counting too quickly or too slowly.

Another knock on the door startles me for the second time, and I manage to choke out a quick, "Yes?"

"Sweetheart, do you want me to save you some dinner?" My mom's voice sounds strained, like she's trying to sound casual, but she's worried. A night where I don't come out of my room to talk off everyone's ear about what's going on at work is rare.

"No thanks, Mom. Not tonight." I probably tried as hard as she did to sound casual before picking up my phone again and dialing Deb Larson.

Nobody answers the phone if they don't recognize the incoming number, so I'm not surprised when the voice mail picks up. "Hi, this is Samantha White, Jax's English teacher from Shipman High School. I just wanted to say how sorry I am for your loss and how much of a loss it is to all of us. Jax was truly special, and I'm sorry he's gone. Please feel free to give me a call back."

I hang up the phone, lay back down, and fall asleep again.

It's almost 2:00 A.M. when I wake up again, groggy and tired. I know there's no way I'll be able to hold myself together at work, so I try to remember how to request a substitute teacher. I've never done it, so I'm a little worried. I'm especially worried because it's 2:00 A.M., and I know Amy will have to find people to cover my classes all day. It doesn't give her much time to do her job.

I pull up the four different websites I'll need to request an absence. One for the district to track my sick days, one for the website that searches for substitute teachers, one for Google Classroom to post some sort of lesson plan for the students while I'm gone, and one to email Amy and Ms. Morris to inform them I'll be out. Within an hour, I notified everyone who needed to be told and posted a scavenger hunt on Shakespeare for my sub-plan. It's moments like this that I wish I had a laptop.

I wonder how substitute teaching plans work with the two-week minimum requirement for community input. Is there a loophole for teacher absences? Because there's no way any substitute teacher is going to do the lesson I had planned on the prologue of Romeo and Juliet. In fact, teacher absences are rampant, and the substitute teacher shortage is so severe that it's usually fellow teachers covering each other's classes. And, since we're giving up our prep periods to do it, there's sort of this unspoken rule that students work independently whenever there's a substitute so the covering teacher can still get some grading and planning done.

With my professional responsibilities finally taken care of, I lay back down and let the exhaustion and sorrow wash over me until I'm asleep again.

The next time I awake, It's the following morning, and my mom is knocking softly on my bedroom door.

"Sam, sweetie, can I come in?" she asks, her voice just above a whisper as if she didn't want to risk waking me.

I clear my dry throat and manage, "Come in."

My mom enters the room, and her beautiful red hair is in curls around her shoulders, making her seem younger than 55 years of age. She carries a tray with a cup of coffee, a plate of scrambled eggs, and a bagel. She knows something is going on but doesn't pry or push. She just shows up and holds space for people when they need it.

She sits on the edge of my bed, and I pull my tired body into a sitting position. The smells of the toasted bagel and hot coffee make my stomach ache in yearning. It's been at least 24 hours since I've eaten anything, and I'm grateful for my mom.

"Thank you," I say quietly, not meeting her eyes. I grab the cup of coffee from the tray she's set on my bed and hold it in my hands, hoping the warmth will radiate through the rest of my body. Maybe this dark cold I'm feeling can be chased away with coffee...

She leans over and kisses me on the head. She turns to leave, but stops when she notices Malcom Mushroom sitting on my bed. Malcom Mushroom only comes out for the very worst afflictions. Seeing the Squishmallow, she sits on the comfy chair beside my bed.

"Samantha, what happened?" Her voice is soft and motherly. It's comforting like honey in a hot cup of tea, easing a sore throat. Her voice soothes my body, and the tears start streaming again. I was trying so hard not to think about it, but I guess I couldn't avoid dealing with it forever.

"A student died," I say through the torrent of tears. My voice is shaky and thin, just like my body feels.

"Oh honey," she says, reaching out her freckled hand and touching my arm. "Was it a student of yours?"

I nod and then start sobbing. My mom moves the tray of food and sits next to me, wrapping her arms around me as I cry.

And then I tell my mom everything. I tell her about the school's new policies and how hard it has been to keep up with them. I tell her about how late I've been staying up to work on lesson plans and grading. I tell her about Jax and Sabrina and the Pride Alliance club. I tell her about Jax's childhood and journey to discover his identity.

I tell her about the Google Form I filled out last week about Jax being transgender and how I haven't seen Jax since. The sobbing takes over again, and I can't get any more words out. My mom just keeps hugging me and smoothing my hair back. She smells like fabric softener and lavender. When I inhale her scent, I'm reminded of the last time she held me while I sobbed this hard.

Stacy.

Once I've exhausted my story, my mom inches the plate of scrambled eggs towards me and looks at me hopefully. I pick up the fork and take a small bite of the food, but it feels like a betrayal. Eating when I feel this sad feels like I'm betraying my body. It doesn't want sustenance. It wants to sleep indefinitely and ignore the world.

"Sam, it's not your fault." Her voice is soft, barely above a whisper. Somehow, it makes it seem louder.

"I know…" I say, trying to sound convincing.

"You couldn't have prevented it."

I finally meet her eyes for the first time since we started talking and retort, "You can't know that."

She frowns, and I can see the pain in her face.

"Sam, if you hadn't reported it, another teacher would have. If Jax asked you to inform his peers of his pronouns, he probably did that in other classes too. If you hadn't reported it, someone else would have."

"Mom, I know it had something to do with Jax's suicide. I just know it. I have this gut feeling that Jax would still be here if I hadn't reported it."

"Sam, even if you hadn't reported it, someone else would have. The ending would have been the same."

I pull out of her embrace entirely now.

"You don't know that!" My voice is loud and shocks even me. "You don't know that another teacher would have reported it. You don't know that he would have still killed himself if it hadn't been reported." I'm seething with anger now, and I'm outraged that my mother doesn't see my role in Jax's death.

"Have you scheduled an appointment with your therapist or psychiatrist yet?" my mom asks.

I shake my head and pick up my cell phone to text my therapist.

"I didn't even think about it," I tell her.

"Well, this is going to be triggering for you. This is going to trigger the same emotions and experiences you had when

Stacy died. And that's okay."

I nod mindlessly, my thoughts somewhere else entirely. At work. At my evaluation.

Oh, crap.

I drop my phone and let my head fall into my hands. I had forgotten entirely about the evaluation. Not that it matters at this point. I'm not sure I even want to go back to work.

How do I work at a school where I'm required to report transgender kids? How do I work at a school where I can't discuss the inappropriateness of students calling each other "gay" as an insult? How do I go back to work and *not* discuss mental health with my students when it feels like it's the *only* thing that matters right now?

"Sam, I have to get to work, but I wanted to make sure you were alright." I can hear the regret in her voice, so I lift my head and put on the best smile I can manage and say, "Thanks, Mom. I'm okay. I'll call Dr. Wright today."

She pulls me close for one last embrace before standing up and leaving for work. She closes the door behind her, so I'm left alone with my plate of slightly picked-at food and intrusive thoughts.

My dad was right. I am way too sensitive to be a teacher. I don't know how to put my emotions aside when I'm in the classroom. I don't know how to avoid conversations about mental health while still getting to know my students and building relationships with them. I don't know how to separate my desire to support students with my desire to teach, and I wonder how other schools do it.

I know more conservative states adopted some of these policies years ago, but it seemed highly unlikely they would make their way to the west coast. I don't know any other teachers dealing with these same struggles. And I really doubt there's a Facebook group called "Teachers In Schools With 'Don't Say Gay' Policies That Disagree".

This wasn't something I was prepared for.

Although, how could I have prepared for this?

Stacy prepared me for this.

I don't think I can be a teacher if I can't help Stacy, if I can't be the teacher Stacy needed...

Maybe I shouldn't have gone into teaching...

24

I'm able to get an appointment with my therapist that same day, and I manage to get my psychiatrist to fit me in the following day. I'm worried about missing my evaluation, but given that I'm currently questioning my entire career choice, it's not at the top of my priority list.

I've been seeing my therapist for years—since Stacy died. I hardly ever see her anymore, but this seems an appropriate time to make an appointment. When I get to her office, my face is still puffy and swollen from the crying. For a brief moment, I miss the mask mandates. I keep my head down while I walk in, hoping no one will notice my blotchy, tear-stained face.

I sign in with the secretary and only wait a moment before my therapist, Linda, invites me back. As soon as we cross the threshold into her office, I'm transported back to when Stacy died. Linda's practice is in the same office in the same building it was all those years ago. Her office is almost the same, with a few pictures being switched out and additional degrees and certifications added to the wall.

I sit on the plump, overstuffed, maroon couch opposite her white sitting chair and avoid her gaze. I fidget with my keys in my lap until she situates herself and says, "So, Sam, how have you been?"

The lump in my throat makes it hard to swallow, but I try anyway. I clear my throat and say, "Not great." When I look up, Linda's wearing a deeply concerned look, and I crumble beneath her gaze. Tears stream down my cheeks like they've been doing all day, and I wonder how I'm not dehydrated yet.

"One of my students killed himself last weekend," I choke out.

"Oh, Samantha, I am so, so incredibly sorry to hear that."

"You know those bills and laws they started calling the 'Don't Say Gay' laws?"

Linda nods in confirmation, and I continue.

"Well, the school that hired me decided to implement some of those things as school-wide, soon to be district-wide, policies. And I didn't know. I had no idea this could happen in our state."

I can tell by Linda's confused look that she's trying hard to empathize with me but has no idea what I'm talking about.

"We're not allowed to have any mental health related conversations with students, and if we learn they're transgender, we're supposed to report it so their families can be investigated for abuse. Well, one of my students told me his pronouns were changing, and I reported it. Next thing I know, I'm being escorted to the principal's office and informed that the same student killed himself."

"Oh, wow, Sam."

She hands me a box of tissues, and I frantically take one and wipe my face.

"I reported him, and he killed himself," I say again. My voice is so quiet that I wonder if she even heard me.

"It's not your fault."

"You don't know that."

"It's no one's fault, Samantha. He made a choice. A painful, sad choice, but a choice nonetheless."

I want to believe her to alleviate some of the guilt I'm

feeling, but I don't believe I was powerless. I don't think anyone is powerless. Everyone had an opportunity to help Jax, to save Jax.

"You couldn't have saved him, Samantha." My eyes meet hers directly for a moment, and she tells me, "And you couldn't have saved Stacy."

The flood of tears seems to start anew, and I'm practically hugging the box of tissues now.

"What if I hadn't reported it? What if he… were alive?" My voice is hoarse now from all the crying.

"He had a whole life before you met him, Samantha. He had a whole history that helped shape who he was and his final decision. Your one decision to follow your job requirements is not the cause of this young man's death."

I nod and think about it. When she puts it that way, it does sound a little silly to think that filling out that Google Form directly resulted in Jax's suicide.

"I don't know if I can keep teaching," I say in a whisper.

"Maybe you should take a few weeks off while you process everything. Your psychiatrist can set you up to take a few weeks off with FMLA."

This sounds like a perfect idea. I can't imagine going back to campus tomorrow. I can't imagine teaching Shakespeare like nothing happened. Ugh. I can't imagine teaching Romeo and Juliet's suicides like nothing happened. How am I going to make it through the year? I think I'm more of a mess than when I started teaching in August.

I spend the rest of my therapy session with Linda discussing my general anxiety and how often I have panic attacks. We discuss breathing techniques, and she suggests I wear a rubber band around my wrist for a while. Each time I look at the rubber band, I'll be reminded to focus on my breathing. If I'm breathing calmly, I can't have a panic attack.

When I returned home, I found an email forwarded by Mr. Sanders with the information for Jax's funeral. Jax's funeral will be this Sunday morning at a nearby church and all are apparently welcome to attend.

At this point, I'm starting to feel numb. I don't have any tears left to cry. I quickly undress and slide back under the covers of my bed, fully prepared to sleep until the sadness dissipates.

Sunday morning, I drag my tired, heavy body out of bed. I pull on an unremarkable black dress and skip the makeup. I figure running mascara would only add to the train-wreck people currently get to see—with my face puffy and swollen from all the crying.

When I arrive at the church, I pull into a parking space at the edge of the parking lot and turn my truck off. I let my head fall back against the headrest and close my eyes. Can I do this? Can I go to a student's funeral alone without a massive panic attack?

"No way," I say out loud to no one. I dig through my tiny purse and take the emergency Xanax I have hidden away. I don't know how to do this. I don't know how to go to a funeral. The last funeral I was at was Stacy's...

The ugly rubber band on my wrist catches my attention, and I remember to breathe. If I'm breathing calmly, I can't have a panic attack. I do my 4-7-8 breathing for a few moments. God, I can't imagine how Jax's... mom is. Mom? Foster mom? Stepmom? I can't imagine how Jax's family is making it through this. I can't imagine how they even planned this in less than a week with all the grief they've been dealing with.

I stuff my keys in my tiny purse, check that my face is no longer red and blotchy from all the crying, and bravely hop out of my truck. I keep my eyes on the ground, afraid I might have to make eye contact and then have a civilized conversation with another human being.

Inside the church, I sit in the last pew, closest to the door. A decade of anxiety has taught me always to choose the seat with the best exit strategy. Closest to the door means I can leave without making a scene. It also means that I can more easily avoid talking to people.

I watch as people slowly filter into the tiny sanctuary. Since I'm sitting in the back row, I see each person as they enter, but only their backs as they walk towards the front of the room. I see several young people enter, arms linked, and recognize one of them as Erin. I haven't seen any students in about a week since I learned of Jax's passing on Monday. I wonder what they must be thinking…

My psychiatrist helped me get a few weeks off from work, but I haven't yet told the students I won't be returning for a while. Penny and my administrators are the only ones I've told. Apparently, I'm excused from any work duties, but Penny has already asked me to keep my Google Classroom up to date. And since I'm not planning on returning for the fourth quarter, I feel like it's the least I can do.

Within 15 minutes, everyone seems to have arrived. There are only about 25 people, and I recognize several of them. Most are teenagers, probably here to mourn their friend. I remember Jax's guardian, Deb, from the Back to School Meet & Greet. She sits in the first row of pews with Erin and several other teenagers.

When the pastor gets up to speak, I'm surprised by how young he is. I'm also surprised that the funeral for a transgender person is being held in a church. And then I start wondering where non-religious people have funerals. I didn't know Jax was religious at all. It wasn't something that ever came up in conversation, and now my mind is running through images of Jax sitting in a pew, Jax at Sunday School as a child, Jax kneeling in prayer in his ripped jeans, and multiple piercings, Jax alive…

My eyes sting, and I can't stop the new onslaught of tears. I squeeze my eyes shut to hold off the tears for as long as possible, and I feel someone sit down next to me on the pew. My eyes open in surprise, and I see Giselle sitting next to me.

Her face has the same motherly concern I've come to expect from people over the last week. She takes my hand and squeezes it. The kindness in her gesture is the tipping point for me, and I start silently bawling. Giselle scoots closer to me and puts her arm around my shoulders.

"Good morning, family and friends," the young pastor's voice fills the large room, making it seem less empty. My eyes scan the front of the room until I spot the casket. Jax's casket.

Jax is in that casket.

No, Jax is gone. There is a body in that casket, but it's not Jax.

The pastor talks briefly about Jax as a young person but spends a good 45 minutes using the time to convince the attendees that they need Jesus. When he's finished with his last offer of unwanted salvation, he sits off to the side.

Deb then walks up to the microphone and, with fumbling fingers, opens the folded paper she clutches tightly in her hands. The awkward rustling of the paper amplified by the microphone is the only sound. Its harshness rips through the silence almost painfully. Something about it all feels so... appropriate. As if harsh sounds and screaming are the only things my heart could handle hearing right now.

At Stacy's funeral, I remember hanging on to every word like it would be the last word I'd ever hear about her. I remember comparing the things her mom said about her to the real Stacy I knew and knowing that no one else in that room knew Stacy as well as I did. But... I didn't think she would kill herself, so maybe I never knew her that well.

By the time my mind returns to the present, I've missed the entire eulogy. Giselle is still holding my hand, and the pastor instructs everyone where the cemetery is located. When I look up at Giselle, she's crying with her eyes closed. She sits, holding my hand, silently crying until I clear my throat. Her eyes popped open as if she had forgotten where she was.

"Would you like to ride to the cemetery with me?" she asks. It's the first words she's spoken to me since sitting down.

I shake my head vigorously. "I can't go. I'm not going." Just thinking about seeing Jax's casket lowered into the ground makes the ache in my chest deep and painful.

"Okay," she says without a hint of judgment. She gives me a quick hug before standing up and leaving.

I follow her out of the sanctuary and into the parking lot. I don't feel the sense of closure or finality I had hoped for. Instead, I feel emptier than before. I cry alone in my truck for a few moments before finally heading home.

25

When I finally return from my leave of absence, two weeks are left in the quarter. I've missed three weeks of school and feel bad about it, but since I'm going to miss the rest of the school year, I don't let myself dwell on it.

I stand at my classroom door to greet students, my hands wrapped around my Dutch Bros. iced coffee. I figured my nerves would be shot by now, but unfortunately, they're still working fine. The butterflies in my stomach are all riled up as I anticipate my conversation with students this morning. I was out for three weeks, but it feels like it's been much longer. I feel like I've forgotten how to talk to my students.

I hear Sabrina shout down the hall, "Miss!" Her face lights up as she runs toward me. She gives me a big hug and says with a wide grin, "You're back! You're back, right?"

I smile half-heartedly and nod, afraid to tell her I won't be back after this quarter. "I am back for today."

"Thank God, I can't stand the substitute teachers. It's so boring and Marie and Isaiah started dating, and they're all over each other during class. It's gross. I'm so glad you're back." Sabrina gives me a quick hug before saying goodbye and heading to her first class.

"Hey, welcome back, Miss," Cody says as he enters the room. He puts his hand out, and I attempt to follow his multi-stepped hand clasp.

"Thanks, it's good to be back," I say cheerfully. Several more students trickle in, many giving handshakes and fist bumps as they enter. Each student that makes a sound of happiness upon seeing me tugs at my heart strings. If I quit teaching, I won't see them anymore. They would have a permanent sub, or more likely—rotating subs—for the rest of the school year.

When the bell finally rings and the last few stragglers have made it into class, I stand in front of my students, sipping my iced coffee and making small talk. Students mostly complain about the teachers covering classes the last few weeks and seem to have zero interest in suddenly getting down to work.

"Alright guys, before we get started today, I wanted to talk to you about a few things," I say nervously.

After Jax's funeral, I thought about all the things I wish I had told him, and it made me want to say those things to all of my students.

"Is it about why you weren't here, Miss?" Cody interjects.

"Sort of…Actually, that's a good place to start. I'm sorry I was gone for so long. I missed you guys a ton, and I'm so glad to be back. I'm not sure how long I'll be back, but I'm happy to be here with you guys today."

"You're not sure how long you'll be back for?" Jasper asks. I was sort of hoping no one would pick up on that little tidbit. I don't want the students to think I will be around longer than I am. It's not fair to them. But I also don't want to talk about *that* at this moment.

"Hold on, hold on," I interrupt him. "Let's focus for a minute on what I wanted to say before I lose my courage. I'm not allowed to talk to you guys about mental health stuff, so I'm kind of nervous."

"Don't worry, Miss. We won't say anything," Cody

interjects again. I flash a quick, appreciative smile at him before I continue.

"I'm not supposed to talk to you about mental health stuff, but our classmate, Jax, took his life. I can't bring Jax back, so it's crucial to me that you guys know how important, special, and loved you are. *You* matter. Who you are…matters. Your story is important. Your story matters. I don't care if it's the happiest story or the saddest tragedy; your story matters.

"I know adolescence is painful. And I know that sometimes that pain feels unbearable, but I promise you it's temporary. It's *all* temporary. Your situation, this life… And you're not alone. I might not be allowed to talk to you about mental health stuff, but your mental health *is* important. If you're feeling depressed or thinking about hurting yourself, please, *please* talk to an adult you can trust. If you don't have any, talk to me, and we'll figure it out."

The kids are silent, but I try to make eye contact with each one at least once. I want each student to feel seen. I *need* each student to feel seen because the world needs fewer teenagers lost to suicide due to modern adults' inability to handle their crap.

"You are all immensely loved," I finish.

Another moment of silence passes, and students stare at me expectantly.

The enigmatic as ever Cody breaks the silence. "Ahh, Miss. We love you too. No cap."

I laugh and say, "Okay, let's talk about Romeo and Juliet! What do you guys think so far?"

We picked up as if I had never left. And since not a single student has read a single word of the play they were supposed to be studying during the last three weeks, it really is like I didn't miss anything at all.

"Come on in, Ms. White," Ms. Morris says warmly. Until today, I had never seen her office, but I like it. It's decorated in a tropical theme with kitschy palm tree leaves and mermaids all over the place. She has a coconut scented candle warming on her desk, adding to the tropical feel.

I sit in the ordinary desk chair facing Ms. Morris and give her a paltry smile. Ms. Morris doesn't know that I'm going to resign, and she's the first person I have to notify to get the process moving. The thought of telling her makes my stomach ache and the butterflies come alive. I wish I had thought to take a Xanax prior to this meeting, but it's too late now.

"I'm going to go over your evaluation with you and then you'll get to ask any questions and sign the form."

"But...I was absent the day I was supposed to be evaluated," I say, unable to hide the concern in my voice.

"You know what, Sam? It's been a long year, you lost a student...I think you've been through enough this year. And anyway, this was supposed to be signed and dated weeks ago—so it's all sort of moot at this point anyway."

"Oh," is all I can manage in response.

"Okay, Ms. White. Here is your evaluation."

Ms. Morris slides a stapled set of papers towards me and I pick them up to look at them. Various numbers are in various colored squares with math I don't want to try to understand. Since I'm no planning on returning to teaching, it doesn't bother me that I have areas for improvement. Good teachers always have room for improvement...but I'm only going to be a teacher for a little while longer.

"Do you have any questions?"

I shake my head, flip to the last page, then sign next to my name. I see the spot next to my name has been retroactively dated to the original date of my observation. Glad to see these documents are fudge-able.

"I do need to let you know..." My heart is pounding and my tongue feels heavy. Am I making a mistake? "I would like to resign at the end of the third quarter," I finally say.

"Oh..." Her face is serious now, and the warmth in her voice has disappeared. She's visibly irritated. "Why?"

"Well, I don't think teaching is the right career for me." S

"Oh, but it's your first year. The first year of anything is always the hardest," her voice is warm and encouraging again, as if she had thought for a brief moment my desire to resign had to do with her or Shipman High. Although in a way, it kind of does…

"It is, that's true…" My voice is shaky, like my resolve, and I continue on, "I don't know how to navigate the political waters of teaching."

"Nobody does. We're all just figuring it out as we go. Building the plane while we are flying it. That's just how education is. It's constant uncertainty and change."

"I am barely learning to fly, Ms. Morris. I don't think I can build the plane *while* I'm learning to fly."

"If it helps, you would have a co-pilot next year."

"What do you mean?" My interest is piqued.

She clicks around on her computer for a moment before continuing. "It looks like you would be teaching English 9 again next year, but you'd have 3 sections of co-taught English 9 with Ms. Hawkins."

I could have a co-teacher! Giselle could be my co-teacher!

"Can I think about it?" I ask hopefully.

"Sure, but Ms. White, I need to know if I need to fill your position for fourth quarter. That really puts us in a tough position. But you gotta do what you gotta do."

"I understand," I say. "I'll make a decision by Friday."

26

I knock lightly on Giselle's propped-open door and see her sitting around with a group of students, listening intently as they talk. She smiles and waves me in. I walk over to her desk and wait for her to join me.

"Sam, hi. Welcome back. How's it going?"

"Good, good. I wanted to tell you I was planning on quitting at the end of the quarter, but Ms. Morris says we'd get to teach together next year if I stay. Did she tell you about that?"

"Yeah, yeah, she did. She asked if I had any preferences for co-teachers, and I offered to mentor you. I hope that's alright."

"Yes!" I'm so excited that somebody *wants* to mentor me and teach with me. I wonder how much easier this year would have been if I had a mentor. "I've never co-taught before."

"Since this is your first year of teaching, I am shocked to hear that!" She says sarcastically with a smile. "Are you quitting, then? Are you leaving Shipman?"

"I don't think I'm cut out to be a teacher," I say, not meeting her eyes.

"What do you mean?"

"Well, it's been a rough year. I filled out a Google Form about Jax being transgender just before he killed himself. I'll never know if it contributed to his suicide, and maybe that's part of the problem. I can't work someplace where I have to report kids' gender identities."

Giselle nods along as I speak. "I totally get it. It's hard. There's no clear rule book on how to navigate political stuff in education. There's no one to tell us how to implement new policies, avoid policies with terrible consequences, or navigate interacting daily with 180 independent teenagers with their own minds, making their own choices.

"We can do our best to follow the school guidelines and district policies, but at the end of the day—students are going to do what they want. If they want to announce their gender identity, they're going to. If they want to leave class, they're going to. If they want to do their work, they're going to. Our job is to be present, guide, teach, and support them. I think you're pretty good at doing that."

"Thanks…" My voice sounds as sheepish as I feel.

"If you really don't want to teach, then you shouldn't be a teacher. It's an extremely demanding profession—mentally, emotionally, and some days physically. So if you're not sure you want to teach, then maybe you shouldn't."

The truth in her words feels harsh, but I know she's right. Teaching is a challenging career; I shouldn't do it if I'm not 100% sure I want to teach.

But I am sure.

I do want to teach. I don't want to report transgender students or dismiss students who confide in me about their mental health. I want to teach sentence structure and Romeo and Juliet. Still, I also want to be able to explain why it's okay to use 'they' pronouns for a single person and tell my students and remind them that their life and individual stories and experiences matter.

"I want to teach. I want to be a teacher. I don't want

ridiculous policies forcing me to choose between following my ethics or my job requirements."

"Sam, these policies are going to come and go. Principals are going to come and go. Every year there will be another administrator, another program, another curriculum, another 'Hail Mary' for whatever ails society and education. There will always be some new initiative to 'help' students that require teachers to push back. Teachers are the ones in classrooms all day with these kids—sometimes we know better than the policy-makers.

"So here's the advice I would offer: put teaching and your students first. Don't worry about the rest of it. Teach the standards; support your students. Ignore the extraneous political stuff."

"How do I ignore the policies requiring me to report stuff?" I ask honestly. I'm having a hard time understanding her confidence. She seems so cavalier about all of it. It's confusing.

"I just meant that it's a small part of the job, and the policies and politics will change constantly. These policies are annoying, but they aren't forever. They're temporary."

Giselle's use of the word "temporary" causes me to pause. I think back to my conversation with my first-period students this morning. I told them everything was temporary. Everything.

"Do you really think the policies will be gone soon?" I ask hopefully. I don't know if this is the deciding factor on whether or not I quit teaching, but it still matters to me.

"You know, with everything going on in our world and Roe V. Wade being overturned…I really don't know. But I know my LGBTQ+ students need trustworthy adults in education more than ever now."

She's right. These policies may or may not continue, but even the ACLU was clear about the current and upcoming attacks on the LGBTQ+ community. I couldn't save Stacy, and I couldn't save Jax. Maybe I can't *save* anyone, but perhaps I *can* be that one supportive adult in a kid's life that significantly reduces their risk of suicide and self-harm.

"I think I cry too much to be a teacher," I say, looking down at my fingers while I fidget nervously.

Giselle laughs and says, "No, you're right on track for the first year of teaching. I promise you'll cry a little less each year than the year before."

I'm not sure I like the sound of that, and my face wrinkles up in disgust as a result. Giselle just laughs.

Giselle and I talk for another few minutes until I've made up my mind on what to do. With my decision made up, I walk determinedly to the front office.

Ms. Morris' office door is closed when I arrive. Laminated cutouts of tropical flowers I can't name cover her entire door. I knock on the laminated flowers hard, hoping she'll be able to hear my knock through all the padding. The butterflies in my stomach start becoming active again. I hate knocking on closed office doors. It feels like such an intrusion—like I just couldn't figure out that a closed door means the person inside is unavailable.

Nobody answers, and I'm disappointed at the anticlimactic result. I leave her office and return to my classroom to compose an email.

I sit at my desk and type up the following:

Ms. Morris,

After careful consideration, I have decided to stay at Shipman High for another year.

Thank you for your time.

Samantha White

www.ingramcontent.com/pod-product-compliance
Lightning Source LLC
Chambersburg PA
CBHW051955150726
47999CB00004B/1396